Claiming the Cowgirl

A NOVELLA

COLORADO COWGIRLS
BOOK FIVE

JODY HEDLUND

BOOKS BY JODY HEDLUND

Colorado Cowgirls

Committing to the Cowgirl
Cherishing the Cowgirl
Convincing the Cowgirl
Captivated by the Cowgirl
Claiming the Cowgirl: A Novella

Colorado Cowboys

A Cowboy for Keeps
The Heart of a Cowboy
To Tame a Cowboy
Falling for the Cowgirl
The Last Chance Cowboy

Healing Springs Ranch

Spurs and Sparks
Broncos and Ballads

Noble Ranch

The Forever Cowboy
The Favored Cowboy

High Country Ranch

Waiting for the Rancher
Willing to Wed the Rancher
A Wife for the Rancher
Wrangling the Wandering Rancher
Wishing for the Rancher's Love

A Shanahan Match

Calling on the Matchmaker

Saved by the Matchmaker
A Wager with the Matchmaker
Marrying the Matchmaker

Bride Ships: New Voyages
Finally His Bride
His Treasured Bride
His Perfect Bride
His Unforgettable Bride

Bride Ships Series
A Reluctant Bride
The Runaway Bride
A Bride of Convenience
Almost a Bride

Orphan Train Series
An Awakened Heart: A Novella
With You Always
Together Forever
Searching for You

Beacons of Hope Series
Out of the Storm: A Novella
Love Unexpected
Hearts Made Whole
Undaunted Hope
Forever Safe
Never Forget

Hearts of Faith Collection
The Preacher's Bride
The Doctor's Lady
Rebellious Heart

Michigan Brides Collection
Unending Devotion
A Noble Groom
Captured by Love

Historical
Luther and Katharina
Newton & Polly

Knights of Brethren Series
Enamored
Entwined
Ensnared
Enriched
Enflamed
Entrusted

Fairest Maidens Series
Beholden
Beguiled
Besotted

Lost Princesses Series
Always: Prequel Novella
Evermore
Foremost
Hereafter

Noble Knights Series
The Vow: Prequel Novella
An Uncertain Choice
A Daring Sacrifice
For Love & Honor
A Loyal Heart

Claiming the Cowgirl

Northern Lights Press

© 2023 by Jody Hedlund

Paperback ISBN: 979-8-9896277-9-0

Jody Hedlund www.jodyhedlund.com

Scripture quotations are taken from the King James Version of the Bible.

This is a work of historical reconstruction; the appearances of certain historical figures are accordingly inevitable. All other characters are products of the author's imagination. Any resemblance to actual events or locales or persons, living or dead, is entirely coincidental.

Cover Design by Roseanna White Designs

Cover images from Shutterstock

One

Fairplay, Colorado
December 1878

She had to stop procrastinating and force herself to pick a new husband.

Serena Taylor tucked her list of potential husbands into the pocket of her day dress. She'd crossed out all but four of the men who lived in the Fairplay area. But maybe just four was narrowing her choice too much?

The bitter December wind coming off the mountains swirled around her, and she hugged Tate closer to protect his plump cheeks from the chill. Burrowing against her chest, he sucked his thumb, content to ride on her hip for as long as she could carry him—which were shorter periods now that he was two and growing bigger every day.

"Only one more visit," she whispered against his forehead before brushing a kiss to his silky light brown hair that was a shade fairer than hers. "Then we'll head home."

Home? She hadn't had a home since running away two months ago from Stony Creek Ranch near Pueblo. Even then, the large spread hadn't felt like home in the few years she'd lived there with Palmer and his parents. It had felt even less so after her husband's death this past summer. In fact, life there had become oppressive—so much so that she'd decided to move back to Oklahoma and live with her family.

She hadn't anticipated that her father-in-law would not only agree that she move away but require her to relinquish her rights to Tate and let him raise her child. When she'd protested, Mr. Halifax's solicitor had presented her with a legal document claiming that a single woman was an unfit mother, mentally unstable, financially irresponsible, and unable to raise a child.

Mr. Halifax was a hard man who always got what he wanted one way or another. So, with only as much of her belongings as would fit into a carpetbag, Serena had ridden away in the middle of the night, afraid that if she stayed even one more day, she'd never see Tate again.

She hadn't known where to go, just that she couldn't return to Oklahoma since it would be the first place Mr. Halifax would look for her. So, she'd traveled to the South Park area until she'd reached Fairplay, and her money had run out.

At least the Courtney Boardinghouse had been a safe haven for the past weeks she'd lived there, working to earn her room and board.

But as she'd learned early in life, all good things had to come to an end eventually. And she couldn't stay at the boardinghouse indefinitely. Not if she hoped to keep Tate. No, she had to stop putting off the one thing that could alleviate all her worries about losing him to Palmer's parents. She had to get remarried. And the sooner, the better.

Serena straightened her petite frame and squared her shoulders, then started down the boardwalk of Fairplay's business district, heading to her final destination and the fourth candidate on her list—Mr. Dankworth, the owner of the mercantile at the end of Main Street. He was a widower with several small children and seemed like a good father.

A good father. That was her number one qualification for a husband. She didn't care how he treated her. As long as he cared about Tate, that's all that mattered.

Well, of course, she also wanted him to be a God-fearing, upright, and law-abiding man. He had to be able to provide financially for her and Tate so that Mr. Halifax would have no reason to question whether Tate's every need was being met.

Her father-in-law was powerful and wealthy, with enough connections that he would learn of her whereabouts eventually—if he hadn't already. And although the mountain passes were now covered in snow and made traveling difficult, Mr. Halifax wouldn't let that stop him from tracking her to the high country.

Hopefully, once she was legally remarried, her father-in-law's accusations would no longer have any merit. At least then her new husband could help her keep custody of Tate.

In the late afternoon, Fairplay's streets weren't yet busy with miners and mill employees who would soon finish work and head to their boardinghouses and the saloons. Even so, the rattle of passing wagons and the clatter of horses mingled with the calls and greetings of the townspeople—mostly men—milling about.

At least she hadn't faced a shortage of marriageable options. In this mountainous area miles from the big cities, men outnumbered women by far. Although Fairplay was a thriving town and had some families, as a single, widowed woman she'd attracted plenty of male attention.

Of course, she needed the right man and couldn't just settle for anyone, which was why she'd been so carefully whittling her list down over recent weeks. The men on her list obviously hadn't realized the so-called chance encounters were interviews, but with each trip into town, she'd purposefully orchestrated time with the candidates so she could get to know them better and see how they interacted with Tate.

Now, with only four remaining on the list, she'd done the same today. She'd coordinated the meetings with each and had only Mr. Dankworth left.

When she finished visiting him, would she finally be able to make her choice?

With her boots tapping firmly against the wooden plank boardwalk, she neared the two-story false storefront with the name *Dankworth's* painted in bold letters above the wooden awning.

Her arms had begun to ache from carrying Tate, but once she reached the interior, she'd set him down as she browsed the wares she couldn't afford and wouldn't be purchasing. Hopefully, Mr. Dankworth would come out from behind his counter and talk to her as he had the past several times she'd stopped in. His oldest daughter, who appeared to be about eight years old, took care of her siblings and had been kind to Tate. Would Mr. Dankworth's children welcome a new brother into their family?

At the door, she paused and straightened her hat—a Gainsborough with round crown and a brim turned up on one side. Navy blue and trimmed with flowers, it was starting to grow shabby, just like the rest of the few garments she'd brought along.

Lifting her chin in resolve, she opened the door to the scent of leather and tobacco as well as the welcoming warmth emanating from the potbellied stove at the center of the store, a coal bin and spittoon beside it.

Floor-to-ceiling shelves lined most walls and were crammed with every conceivable item—canned foods, spices, crockery, fabric, sewing notions, and medicines. The countertops ran the length of one side, and they were piled with ready-made clothing, blankets, hats, and more. Horse whips and farming tools hung from the ceiling.

Several other customers were in the store: an older man near the back examining harnesses, a fellow sitting in a chair near the stove and reading a newspaper, and another man at the counter—a tall, dark-haired man she immediately recognized.

Weston Oakley. He had lean facial features with a squared jawline, a prominent chin with a noticeable cleft, and a nose with a slight dorsal bump. His coat stretched tightly across his broad shoulders and thickly-muscled arms. And his torso and legs radiated equal strength, although his wool trousers hung more loosely and were tucked into worn leather boots.

"My family doesn't think I'm capable of getting married," Weston was saying. "And if I don't round up a wife by Christmas, they'll never leave me alone."

The very handsome Weston Oakley had recently belonged to Felicity Courtney. Perhaps *belonged* wasn't the right word, but the two had been nearly engaged. The rumor was that Weston had even built a house for her.

However, Felicity had broken Weston's heart when she'd married someone else and moved away.

Serena liked Felicity. After all, Felicity had been the one running the boardinghouse and had taken her in during her time of need.

But Serena wished Felicity hadn't hurt Weston so terribly. She hadn't been fair to the kind, hard-working man. Although Serena had contemplated making him number five on her list of potential husbands, she'd witnessed firsthand the heartache he'd experienced from Felicity's rejection, and she'd seen the misery in his expression ever since.

She'd concluded that he wasn't ready to form another relationship so soon after losing Felicity. But what if she was wrong?

As the door closed behind her and she stepped farther into the store, every eye shifted her way, including Mr. Dankworth's and Weston's.

"Good afternoon, Mrs. Taylor." Mr. Dankworth stood suddenly straighter, adjusting his bow tie and collar before slicking back his thinning brown hair. On the shorter side of average, Mr. Dankworth wore an apron over his suit, which seemed overly large on his trim frame.

"Ma'am." Though Weston nodded at her politely, his blue-black eyes flitted over her and dismissed her all in one motion—just as usual.

Also just as usual, his gaze came to rest on Tate.

The boy lifted his head from her shoulder and slid his thumb out of his mouth. Now he was staring at Weston with his wide green eyes—the color another trait she and Tate shared.

"Hey there, little fella." Weston offered Tate a tender smile.

"Ball?" Tate asked timidly.

Serena lowered Tate to the ground. He promptly latched on to her skirt, clinging to her as he always did whenever they were around other people. She had to stifle the urge to flex her arms and stretch the ache out of her back.

"Sorry." Weston stuffed his hands in his pockets. "I don't have a ball today."

The last time she and Tate had encountered Weston was several days ago at church. When Tate had gotten restless during the service, Weston, from the pew behind them, had handed Tate a marble to play with.

She'd been grateful for Weston's consideration, especially when he'd insisted afterward that Tate could keep the marble, since he'd apparently picked it up off the street and had no use for it.

Weston pulled a hand out of his pocket and held out a stick of light-pink candy. "I've got this candy . . . if your ma says it's okay for you to eat."

At the sight of the offering, Tate's beautiful eyes rounded even more. He shifted his questioning gaze up to her. "Candy, Mama?"

How could she say no when his face was filled with such innocence and sweetness? He'd had so few pleasures during his short life—had more frightening experiences than anything. Besides, with the little she earned working at the boardinghouse, she didn't have much to spare for simple gifts.

She brushed his hair out of his eyes. "Alright."

Tate released his grip on her skirt and took a tentative step toward Weston. Then, in a burst, he raced the last of the distance. As he took the stick, Weston ruffled Tate's hair.

"What do you say to the nice man?" Serena prompted.

Tate was already running back to her side, his eyes containing an equal measure of both fright and excitement. As he latched on to her skirt again, she tucked a finger under his chin and leveled stern eyes upon him. "Tell Mr. Oakley *thank you.*"

"Thank you." Tate's voice was so soft she doubted anyone heard him.

But Weston nodded, then gathered up a parcel from the counter, tipped the brim of his black Stetson toward Mr. Dankworth, and crossed to the door, his boots clunking against the wooden floorboards. As he passed by, he ruffled Tate's hair again. "Enjoy the candy, little fella."

Then, with a polite touch of the brim of his hat in farewell to her, he exited the mercantile.

She couldn't keep from watching him through the glass panes on the front door as he crossed the street and seemed to head toward the bank. His stride was long and determined, and he carried himself with strength and purpose, as though the whole world yet needed his conquering.

After his declaration to Mr. Dankworth about needing a wife by Christmas, did she dare turn him into her fifth matrimonial candidate?

He always interacted so thoughtfully with Tate, and Tate seemed to be drawn to him the most, even aside from the gifts of the marble and candy.

Yes, Weston Oakley would most definitely

qualify to be on her list. The question was, would he consider marrying her after his recent heartache? He hardly seemed to realize she existed—probably wouldn't regard her at all if not for Tate.

"What can I do for you today, Mrs. Taylor?" Still behind the counter, Mr. Dankworth had donned a wide and welcoming smile, appreciation lighting up his face as it normally did whenever he looked at her.

Like the other three candidates, he was always eager for her visits, going out of his way to talk with her and pay her compliments. He hadn't yet proposed as the others had, but she predicted it wouldn't be long before he did.

She could have her choice of the four.

But shouldn't she at least test Weston and determine if he was a possibility too?

For a long moment her mind spun, doing what it did so well—scheming and plotting to make circumstances work to her advantage. As an idea began to evolve, she nodded at Mr. Dankworth and turned to the door. "I guess I won't be needing anything today after all. But I do thank you for the offer."

With Tate clinging to her skirt and sucking on his candy, she exited the mercantile. She had to hurry if she had any hope of facilitating a *chance* meeting with Weston before darkness fell.

Hopefully, this time he would take more notice of her and perhaps even consider her a prospect for the wife he needed by Christmas.

Two

"Cold, Mama." Tate wrapped his arms around Serena's leg.

The winter wind buffeted them as they stood on the road north of Fairplay. Miles of grassland, hemmed in by mountain ranges, spread out all around them, forming a valley in Colorado's high country, perfect for the many ranches that made the South Park basin home.

Serena squinted to see down the well-worn wagon path and crossed her fingers for a glimpse of Weston Oakley. But in the fifteen minutes or more they'd been waiting, there hadn't been a single sign of him.

She didn't know if there was another route to his ranch in addition to the winding road that ran along the South Platte River, but it was possible he'd ridden home another way.

"Up." Tate tugged at her skirt with sticky fingers, his candy finally gone. Even with a cap on his head and a warm woolen coat, his nose was rosy from the cold and matched his cheeks. And the December air was growing colder as daylight dissipated.

She didn't want Tate to suffer and would have to set aside her plans for the evening and perhaps try again tomorrow. With a sigh, she stuck two fingers into her mouth to whistle and call back Belle.

But before she could make the sharp sound, a plume of dust whipped by wind rose in the distance. A team pulling a wagon was headed her way. Was a customer riding out to one of Weston's mills to collect lumber or grain? Or was the man himself finally coming?

Just in case it was him, she let her shoulders slump and began to amble along while carrying Tate.

The rumble of the wagon grew more distinct until it wasn't far behind her. She stopped, turned, and waited for the approach. At the sight of Weston's black Stetson, broad shoulders, and thick arms, relief warmed her limbs and gave her renewed energy for her scheme.

When he was almost upon her, he tugged on his reins. "Whoa."

As he halted the team and wagon beside her, she wrapped her arms more firmly around Tate and let herself visibly shudder.

"Mrs. Taylor?" His tone was tight with worry, and he scanned the fields beyond her as though waiting for a wild creature to rush out and attack them. "What are you doing out here this time of the evening?"

She whispered a silent plea for forgiveness for deceiving this good man, but sometimes desperate times required desperate measures. "My horse got away from me, and I headed after her, hoping I could catch her." It was technically the truth, even if she had purposefully let Belle wander off.

He glanced both ways on the wagon path as though he might spot her. "She came north, you think?"

"Yes, I believe so." She nodded down the path ahead that led to his home. "I thought I caught a glimpse of her a few minutes ago. She can't be too far away now."

He searched the barren landscape again. Although the river wasn't visible from the wagon path, the tall cottonwoods and shrubs that lined the waterway stood a short distance away. Beyond them to the west, the foothills began their gentle rise, leading to the majestic peaks crowned with gold and royal blue as the sun faded behind the mountains.

Though the high summits were already snow-covered, South Park's almost-ten-thousand-foot elevation didn't have a covering of snow—at least, not one that stayed beyond a day or two. As the cold wind slapped her again, she didn't have to fake her next shudder.

In the next instant, Weston was hopping off the wagon bench to the ground. "Reckon you better let me take you home, ma'am."

"Oh, I couldn't trouble you." She made sure to emphasize her Southern accent, since it often worked in her favor.

He took a step toward her. "I don't mind none."

She paused as though to consider his offer. Then she shook her head. "I'm sure Belle isn't far."

"She's probably halfway back to the boardinghouse by now."

So, he did know where she lived. What else did he know about her? "I'm fairly certain she's just around the corner ahead." Serena started walking but made it only three steps before his footsteps crunched against the ground and he stopped her with a touch to her arm.

"No sense in walking." He drew back, his forehead furrowed. "I'm headed up the road and can give you a ride."

She hesitated. "Are you certain I won't be a bother?"

"Not a bit."

She offered him a tenuous smile. "Then thank you. Tate's tired, and he's not as easy to carry as he once was."

"Reckon it won't be long before he learns to ride." Weston led the way to the wagon.

She wanted to protest that her son was too young, but she'd been riding herself when she was but a girl of three. "He already loves horses, don't you, Tate?"

The little boy nodded, having lifted his head to watch Weston's every move. Now, as the handsome man took hold of her elbow and guided her up to the wagon bench, she could feel Weston's scrutiny upon them too.

As she positioned herself with Tate on her lap, she visibly shuddered again.

The movement seemed to spur Weston into

action, and he stalked around the wagon to the other side. "Looks like you've been out too long."

"Yes, I'm afraid we're both frozen through." She held her breath. Would he take the hint or not?

"You're welcome to ride on to my house to warm up. It's just a few shakes of a horse tail down the road."

She held back a smile. He'd taken the hint well. "I really don't want to impose. If I find my horse, I'll be fine—"

"I insist." He hopped up and positioned himself next to her. "If you're worried about me, I guarantee I ain't a shady fella. I promise you'll be safe. I've got a housekeeper . . ."

It was her turn to touch his arm, and the brief contact brought his words to a halt. "I'm not worried, Mr. Oakley."

"You're not?" He shifted on the bench, and she could feel his gaze taking her in, perhaps really seeing her for the first time.

This was going well. Just the way she'd hoped. "I haven't been in Fairplay long, but I've learned enough about you to know that you're trustworthy."

"That right?"

"Yes." She fidgeted with wrapping Tate closer,

pretending not to notice Weston's continued scrutiny. Felicity Courtney wouldn't have given Weston a second glance if he hadn't been trustworthy. But now didn't seem the right time to bring up Felicity's name. Not when his hurt over her rejection was still so fresh.

He started his team on their way and then cleared his throat, obviously intending to carry on more conversation.

Good. That's exactly what she wanted.

"What brought you to Fairplay?" he asked.

She'd practiced her answer to those kinds of probing questions before she'd arrived in the high country, knowing she needed to have a story for her sudden appearance as a single woman with a toddler in tow.

So far, she'd tried to stick as close to the truth as possible—that her husband had passed away, she was a widow, and she was hoping to find work. At some point, she would have to reveal the trouble with her father-in-law trying to take Tate from her, but for now, such news was best left unspoken. "I grew up on a ranch and thought this might be the perfect place to start over, since the area has so many ranches."

Weston didn't respond for a beat. The wagon rumbled comfortably down the path, the wilted brown grass cushioning the ride. With the sun sinking even further behind the range and with darkness settling, the air held an almost peaceful aura, like the lull before a storm.

Had her response not been convincing enough? Could he see through her answer? "What about you, Mr. Oakley? What brought you to Fairplay?" The best way to avoid more questions was to take the attention off herself and place it squarely on someone else.

"My family has a ranch up in the Breckenridge area." He held the reins loosely in his gloved hands—hands that were clearly accustomed to hard work. "But I got the itch to strike out on my own eight years ago and came on down here to Fairplay to start my own ranch."

Tate snuggled into her side, now sucking his thumb after having pulled his mittens off. He watched Weston with a fascination that mirrored hers.

"What made you decide to build your lumber and grain mills too?"

Even though Weston had a powerful build and held himself with a rugged confidence, he also seemed comfortable riding and talking with her, as though he made an everyday practice of riding and talking with women. "I like new ventures. Keeps me busy."

Would he like the new venture of gaining a wife and son? More importantly, would he be a truly viable candidate for becoming Tate's father?

She bent and pressed a kiss to Tate's forehead. From the corner of her eye, she could see Weston watching her.

"How long you been a—" He paused. "How long's the boy been without his pa?"

From the tentativeness in his tone, he was likely trying to determine if she was still grieving. Perhaps some widows were reluctant to speak about their former spouses, but she wasn't. She was ashamed to admit she'd never grieved for Palmer—had felt relief more than anything when she'd received news of his death.

"I'm sorry." Weston rushed to speak. "Ain't none of my business."

"It's alright. My husband died in a brawl six months ago." He'd been shot in the head by his mistress's husband, but Serena kept that fact to herself, not wanting to speak ill of Palmer in front of Tate. The boy didn't need to know about his daddy's problems. It was already going to be hard enough to someday explain why she'd left

Palmer's home and family, let alone how he'd died.

"Reckon that wasn't an easy way to lose him." Weston still spoke hesitantly.

"Nothing about my previous husband was particularly easy." She may as well hint that she was ready to move on. Then if he took an interest in her, he didn't have to worry about her harboring feelings for another man.

As the wagon rounded the bend, the mills came into view. Two tall wooden buildings along the river's edge gleamed now in the last glow of the sunset. Stacks of cut lumber surrounded the one closest to them. Gray sacks—likely filled with grain—were stacked on the loading dock of the other mill.

The spacious, cleared yard in front of both buildings was silent and deserted, the workers having gone home for the evening. Now that crops had been harvested, Weston's business was likely slower throughout the winter.

"Don't see a horse anywhere." Weston surveyed the leafless brush along the riverbanks. "Do you?"

She pretended to search too, but she knew well enough that one whistle was all it would take to call Belle from wherever she'd wandered. Belle had been her favorite horse for years, and she'd needed something of her own when she'd moved so far from her childhood home and family.

She shook her head. "I don't see her either."

Tate lifted his head. "Hungry, Mama."

She never went anywhere without snacks and extra clothing for Tate and had brought snacks for him just in case—an apple, a roll, even a pickle. She shifted the bag from her shoulder— the one she'd tucked into the saddlebags but taken out before she'd slapped Belle's hindquarters and sent her on her way.

"My housekeeper will have some vittles ready." Weston spoke before she could find the drawstring on the bag. "You're welcome to have a meal."

"You're already doing enough, Mr. Oakley. I couldn't impose any further."

"You're not imposing. Maude'll be more than happy to have someone else to dote on besides an old scallywag like me."

"I don't know . . ." This *chance* encounter with Weston was going better than she could have predicted. Regardless, she didn't want to lead him on or encourage him unnecessarily. He wasn't yet on her list, although she had every intention of penning his name there the moment she was in her room at the boardinghouse. In fact, she had to admit he was already climbing high on the list, might even already be at the top.

"Maude makes the best biscuits this side of the Divide." Weston reached over and gently bumped Tate's arm with his fist. "You can't leave without trying them, right, little fella?"

Tate nodded vigorously. "Me try."

"Guess it's settled." Weston guided the team down a long lane that ended at a two-story colonial-style house painted a pale yellow, with a wrap-around porch and front windows brightly lit from within. "You'll stay for supper."

"Thank you. That's very kind of you." Truthfully, Weston Oakley was probably on a list all of his own. But she still had to be careful about moving too fast and making quick judgments. One bad marriage had been enough. Even though she didn't have high expectations for the next husband, at least she had the right to choose and didn't have to go along with what her daddy wanted.

Hopefully, this time she'd end up with a better man.

Three

How long had he been dreaming of having a woman sit at the table with him and share a meal?

Weston pushed his empty plate away and reclined in the dining room chair across from Serena Taylor and her boy. He reckoned he'd been wanting it longer than an old-timer waiting to find a mother lode.

"So, now that Charity and Hudson have located a nurse to care for Mr. Keller," she was saying about the invalid at the boardinghouse, "they no longer need my assistance in that manner."

He'd hardly been able to pay attention to their conversation throughout the meal. Not only because Maude had been in and out of the dining room a dozen times, her smile wider than a transatlantic railroad, but also because Tate had needed Serena's attention—everything from cutting up his food into bite-sized pieces to prompting him to use manners.

But the biggest distraction hadn't been Maude or Tate. It had been his own runaway thoughts. About Serena.

Of course he'd noticed her around town over the past weeks since she'd arrived in Fairplay. What man wouldn't notice her? She was too pretty to miss. Her face was dainty, delicately framed with slender lines along her jaw that led to a long, graceful neck and a generous swell of curves that her tight bodice highlighted much too well.

Her hair was plaited in a single braid—not quite the same pale shade as Tate's but a pretty mingling, as if it couldn't quite decide whether to be blond or brown. Her eyes, though, were most definitely green—the green of a forest of lush pine trees.

As fine-looking as she was, he was surprised another man hadn't already gotten his loop around her. It had been plain as day that Mr. Dankworth had caught Cupid's cramp over her.

No doubt the mercantile owner—and a dozen other men—were biding their time for her to be ready for marriage again.

From the few things she'd mentioned about her late husband during the wagon ride to his house, maybe she was already willing to tie another knot.

She wiped Tate's mouth with a napkin. "Of course, Charity is the sweetest woman I've ever met, and she told me I can live at the boardinghouse as long as I want."

"That's mighty nice of her." Had he said the right thing? Or did he sound like a blathering idiot?

"Yes, the Courtney sisters are very nice women—kind, helpful, lovely. I don't know where I'd be if not for Felicity . . ." Her voice trailed off, and she focused intently on Tate's plate, scraping a fork along the edge as if she intended to get every last crumb off even though there was nothing left.

Was she embarrassed to talk about Felicity after what had happened to him? Did Serena think he was pining after the beautiful redhead?

Reckoned if he was honest, he was still sore about Felicity falling for another man so quickly after he'd been trying to court her for months. He could admit, he'd even had the house built with the hope that she'd finally accept one of his proposals.

Worse, he'd been so certain Felicity would marry him that he'd told his entire family on his last visit home a couple of months ago that he'd have a wife by Christmas. They'd scoffed at his words. They all knew his history, that he'd been searching for a wife for years and hadn't had any luck—not even with the matrimonial catalogs or newspaper advertisements.

Of course, he'd had to insist that this time things were different. And he'd vowed to show them that this Christmas he'd finally have a wife by his side when he arrived at the ranch for the holiday.

With Christmas only three weeks away, he was gonna be riding home with his tail tucked between his legs. His family would tease him to no end. But what he dreaded most was the pity. Even if they tried to hold it back, he'd see it, just like he had in the past—those long, meaningful glances that said they were thinking about Electra, his first love, the woman he'd almost married.

No one ever said her name. Even after eight

years, just hearing her name or thinking about her still brought swift pain to his chest.

He wasn't sure how he could face his family's pity one more time. He'd half a mind to skip the Christmas festivities just to avoid the questions . . . and another serious jawing from his pa, which was bound to be more of the same advice to let go of his past and move forward into the future.

Holy high heavens. He'd built a house for a wife. What more could he do to prove he was moving forward into the future?

His pa's words from the last visit echoed in his head. *"When you find the right woman, just make yourself get married this time. Don't come up with any more excuses why you can't."*

"I apologize." Serena was rising from her chair across the table and picking up Tate. "I didn't mean to bring up Felicity. I know it can't be easy . . ."

He stood quickly. What should he say? That the sting wasn't hurting quite as much anymore? That he was doing better? That he was even beginning to realize Felicity might not have been the right woman for him after all?

Serena hefted Tate to her hip and pushed in their chairs. Then she paused, staring at the candles Maude had lit and placed at the center of the otherwise undecorated table. In fact, the entire house was undecorated, with only the most basic of furniture in some of the rooms. Many rooms were still unfurnished.

"Thank you again for coming to our rescue, Mr. Oakley—"

"Weston."

Her gaze shot up to his, her eyes wide and questioning. Was she surprised he was giving her permission to use his given name so soon?

He was surprising himself. "There's no need to apologize for talking about Felicity. I think she married the man she was meant to be with."

Serena nodded, as though agreeing. "Regardless, I know it couldn't have been easy."

"It's my fault for letting my Cupid's cramp get the best of me."

"Cupid's cramp?" Her lips curved into the beginning of a smile.

"Reckon it's a common ailment around these parts for most men."

"Maybe for women too." Her words came out soft and were accompanied by a flush to her cheeks. She buried her nose in Tate's hair as if to hide from her confession.

But it was out there. For the taking. And he didn't quite know what to do with it.

"Well, I'll be going." She started to round the table. "I've got quite a walk ahead of me."

"Whoa now." He stepped into her path. "I won't be letting you walk anywhere tonight, Mrs. Taylor—"

"Serena." She stared at the undone top button of his flannel shirt, clearly embarrassed by her own boldness at permitting him to use her given name.

"Serena." He let the name roll off his tongue. It was pretty.

She didn't make a move to leave. And strangely, he wasn't ready for her to go.

"Weston?" Maude's voice came from directly behind him in the hallway, nearly making him jump.

The native woman had a knack for creeping up on him without notice. He reckoned she must've learned to walk as silently as a cougar during her youth, when she'd hunted with her Ute tribe all throughout the high country.

He shifted and gave his housekeeper his attention—or at least as much as he could, because half of it was still on Serena.

Maude clasped Ranger's collar, holding the black-spotted pointer back from lunging forward in his excitement at being around a rare visitor in the house. "You let the pretty lady and her boy stay here while you go look for her horse." Maude's leathery face was creased with age and her top front teeth were long gone. But her hair hung in two black braids, hardly touched by gray, and her body was still straight and lithe.

She had been a part of his family for years. In fact, he'd been the one to stumble upon her in a mountain cave near their home shortly after they'd moved to Breckenridge after the end of the War of Rebellion.

At first he'd believed Maude had been left for dead by her tribe. But at the faint signs of life within her frail body, he'd taken her home to his ma, who'd nursed her back to health. Maude had stayed with the family ever since. And when he'd said he was moving to Fairplay, she'd informed him she was coming with him.

That was the thing about Maude. She hardly ever asked and almost always told him what to do. Most of the time he didn't mind. He'd gotten used to her bossiness. But when it came to women, he'd always been quick to remind her that he didn't need or want her help.

Tonight was no exception. "The wagon's still hitched. I'll take Mrs. Taylor on home now before it gets too cold, and I'll search for her horse tomorrow."

"You go look now." Maude pinched the back of Ranger's neck and motioned for him to sit, which he promptly did, his tongue lolling out one side of his mouth. "Wolves still roam the plains and are hungry."

"Oh no." Serena's gentle features tightened. "I didn't realize Belle would be in danger, or I would have taken more care with her."

"The horse'll be just fine." Weston shot a warning look at Maude—hopefully one she could read—cautioning her against saying anything more. "With the cooler temperatures, we might have a few wild critters who haven't gone to the lower elevations, but it ain't nothin' to worry about."

Serena's worry clouded her green eyes in spite of his assurance. "I can't let anything happen to her."

"Reckon she's back at the boardinghouse by now, but how about if I take a ride around and see if I spot her?"

"I'll go with you." She started to put Tate down, but the boy tightened his hold around her neck.

Maude was right. He'd be better off having

Serena wait. Even without the little fella, she'd slow down his search, and he'd be able to cover more ground without her. "If I can't find your mare on my land, then I'll take you on back to the boardinghouse, and we can search on the way there."

She nodded reluctantly.

Within minutes he was outside on his way to the barn in the frigid night, bundled in his coat and hat and gloves. He saddled and mounted his gelding, then veered toward the river with Ranger trotting alongside him. As he took a last glance at the house, something strange warmed his insides at the thought of Serena and Tate waiting there for his return.

He didn't know all that much about the widow and her little boy, but he couldn't deny that after spending the past couple hours with her, he wanted to find out more. She was interesting and kind and soft-spoken. And she was also a good mother—he'd noticed that the very first time he'd watched her interact with her boy around town and at church.

But as much as she might intrigue him, he wasn't sure if he was ready to get calico fever again. He'd been hurt one too many times, and his heart couldn't take any more breaking.

Four

Was Weston Oakley the solution to all her problems and the key to keeping Tate?

Serena held Tate in her arms, his eyes closed in slumber and his thumb halfway out of his mouth. She brushed his hair off his forehead and then leaned her head back against the cushioned chair beside the fireplace in Weston's parlor.

Though the room was devoid of furniture and decorations except a simple settee and matching chair, the warmth, quiet, and peace of the house had settled around her, making her drowsy. Maude had kindly brought her a blanket for extra warmth, and Serena was sorely tempted to close her own eyes and let sleep claim her.

But what would Weston say if he returned and found her slumbering? She didn't want him to think she was an incompetent mother—the accusation her father-in-law had leveled at her when he'd told her she could no longer raise Tate as her own.

Deep inside, she knew she wasn't incompetent. She'd been a loving mother since the moment Tate had been born. But her father-in-law had catalogued her every misstep with Tate—everything from how many rashes Tate had suffered to how many nights he'd been up crying. All the allegations had shaken her already rocky confidence—the confidence that had slowly eroded while she'd been married to Palmer.

Even now she couldn't keep from wondering what she'd done wrong as a new wife, why he hadn't been happy and satisfied with her. If she'd tried harder to be what he'd needed, maybe he wouldn't have had a reason to seek out other women.

At the creak of the front door opening and footsteps entering, she sat up. Was Weston returning? There was no clock upon the fireplace mantel to indicate the passing of time, but she guessed not more than half an hour had passed since Weston had ridden out to search for her horse.

She started to stand.

"Howdy, Maude," came an unfamiliar male voice.

Serena sat back down and held herself motionless. She shouldn't be in a single man's home like this. Even with his housekeeper present, it was improper for a woman—even a widow—to fraternize so privately. If people discovered she'd been at his house alone after dark, she'd risk ruining her reputation.

With a tarnished reputation, would any of the men on her suitable-husband list still want her?

"Maverick." Maude's voice held a note of affection. "You surprised me."

"Of course I did," the man replied, humor tinging his voice.

From the shuffling and muffling of Maude's reply, Serena guessed the newcomer was giving the old housekeeper an embrace.

"You stay here for the night," Maude said a moment later.

"Nope, just passing through on my way back home."

"Too late for travel. Dark. Bandits. Wild animals. You must stay."

Maverick gave a soft guffaw. "You know I'll be just fine."

"Then you eat before you go."

"How long before Weston returns?"

Serena wasn't sure how the newcomer knew Weston was gone. Perhaps because Ranger wasn't there to bark a greeting?

"Weston is looking for his wife's horse."

"Wife?" Maverick's question rang with surprise.

It echoed the surprise jabbing at Serena, making her sit up straighter.

Did Maude believe that because Weston had brought her into his home, she was his wife? Or maybe Weston had said something that made Maude think they'd gotten married?

"Wife and son," Maude persisted.

"Really?" Maverick's tone filled with skepticism. "When did this happy occasion occur?"

"Today."

"I won't believe it until I see it."

"She is here now."

"Now?" Maverick's voice dropped to a whisper.

A beat of silence passed. Was Maude nodding her head?

"Well, I'll be hanged." Maverick's whisper was still loud enough for Serena to hear. "Never thought I'd see the day. None of us did."

What did that mean? In the mercantile earlier, Weston had mentioned something about his family not believing he was capable of getting married. Did this have something to do with that? And was Maverick family?

"Last news I heard," Maverick whispered, "the Courtney sister he was pining over got married to someone else."

"I don't know nothing about that." Maude's gravelly attempt at whispering fell short. "This here lady, she's real nice."

Why had Maude decided that Serena was nice? Had the housekeeper eavesdropped during the supper conversation?

Before Serena could determine what to do, a dark-haired man with the same lean facial features, squared jawline, and prominent chin as Weston filled the doorway of the parlor.

Yes, she had no doubt whatsoever that this visitor was Weston's family, possibly a brother. The resemblance was too striking to be otherwise. Not only was he as handsome and muscular, but his eyes held the same intensity.

He was slightly shorter than Weston, and his

eyes were a lighter shade of blue. Those eyes were fixed upon her, widening with every passing second that he took her and Tate in.

Serena needed to clarify that she wasn't married to Weston to both the housekeeper and this man. But Maude was nowhere in sight.

What could Serena possibly say that wouldn't make things go from bad to worse? Already Maverick assumed she was married to Weston. If she denied it, would he assume that she and Weston were having illicit relations?

Lunacy of lunacies. What should she do?

At the very least, she needed to stand and greet the newcomer. That was the polite thing, and she was, after all, still a born and bred Southern woman with manners. She started to scoot to the edge of her chair and push herself up.

But Maverick shook his head and placed a finger over his lips with a meaningful look at Tate—one that said he had no wish to wake her son and that she didn't need to rise on account of him.

Once again, she stayed in the chair, but this time she sat stiffly, her mind racing to find the right explanation that would rectify the situation.

"Nice to meet you, ma'am," Maverick

whispered as he studied her again. "My congratulations on being the woman to finally rope Wes into marriage."

She had to say something. "I apologize, but—"

"Shoot, look at me forgetting proper introductions." Maverick's lips turned up into an easy grin. "I'm Maverick, one of Weston's younger brothers. Obviously much more charming and handsome."

The front door opened again, and this time, the scamper of a dog was followed by Weston's heavy steps.

Maverick backed out of the doorway and into the hallway.

"Thought that was your horse tied up out there," Weston said, his voice filled with welcome.

"Yep. Passing through the area. Was checking into a new stud for one of the broodmares." Several backslaps told her the two brothers were embracing. At Ranger's whining, Serena guessed the dog wanted his share of attention too.

"Maverick met Serena." Maude's claim rose above the clamor.

"Never thought I'd see the day." Maverick had abandoned his whispering, and his tone contained mirth. "But looks like we were all wrong."

"What's new about that?" Weston's quip was good-natured.

"With as many failed attempts, what'd you expect?"

"Failed attempts?"

"The Courtney gal. Was she the fifth or sixth gal you proposed to?"

Serena's pulse was beginning to tick faster. Weston was probably growing more confused with every passing comment. Should she go out into the hallway and intervene so that Weston didn't mistakenly assume she was to blame for the mix-up?

She made it to her feet this time, Tate still blissfully unaware of the turmoil brewing around him.

"Reckon you ain't much better." Though Weston's tone still was light, it held an edge this time. "How long you been courting Hazel? Five or six years?"

"Whoa now." Maverick's tone turned hard. "We ain't courting and never will. We're just friends."

Weston snorted. Then silence descended in

the hallway. And tension. In fact, the tension was so thick Serena could feel it.

"You come eat now." Maude's command cut through the silence. "Weston will go check on his wife."

Serena pulled in a breath. Then she waited for Weston's anger to flare to life. Surely it would now.

Five

Wife? What in the blazes was Maude talking about?

Before he could get the question out, Maude grabbed his arm and propelled him toward the parlor door. "Go now. You talk with Serena first while I feed Maverick."

"Sure, Wes." Maverick's wide grin was back in place. "Go *talk* with your wife."

"Hold on now." Protest rose swiftly inside Weston. But Maude was already shoving him into the parlor, and Serena stood beside a chair near the hearth, Tate asleep in her arms.

Her eyes were wide, almost frightened, and she took a step back.

Obviously she'd heard the part about being his wife. There was no other explanation for her reaction. Not when she'd been so open and friendly with him earlier.

He came to a halt just inside the door and waited as Maverick and Maude moved down the hallway toward the kitchen with Ranger trailing them, his paws thumping against the wood floor. When the kitchen door clicked closed and Maverick's and Maude's voices became muted, Weston took off his Stetson and cleared his throat. "Guess you heard Maude tell my brother you're my wife?"

"Yes. I'm not sure what happened to lead her to believe we're married. I guarantee I didn't say anything." From the distress drawing lines into her delicate forehead and at the corners of her eyes, he knew her answer was sincere, that she wasn't responsible for whatever misunderstanding had taken place during his absence.

If anyone was to blame, it was likely Maude. Even though the old native had learned to speak good English over the years, she didn't always comprehend everything, and they'd had their share of miscommunication.

This miscommunication was a big one, though.

Maverick believed Serena was his wife, and when he returned to the ranch, he'd tell everyone.

Weston twisted his hat. On the one hand, the pressure from family would finally go away. On the other hand, when he showed up at Christmas without the expected wife, he'd only be humiliated more than ever.

Unless . . .

Serena's eyes took on a wariness, as if she could see the wheels in his head rolling faster, picking up momentum.

What if he actually took her to his family's home? Since everyone would already believe they were married, maybe he could convince Serena to spend Christmas with him.

And what? Pretend to be his wife for a few days?

He gave a curt, frustrated shake of his head. He wouldn't be able to deceive his family. And he'd never ask Serena to join him in such deception. Not that she'd even consider it. She seemed like an honest and upright woman.

"I apologize," she whispered. "This is all my fault for being here. I shouldn't have come."

"It's not your fault."

"It really is." She cast her sights down to Tate, her cheeks flushed. "I was interested in meeting you—I mean, I liked how you treated Tate. You're good with him."

She'd been interested in meeting him? Weston's thoughts halted their tumultuous rumbling, and an eerie quiet settled in to replace the noise. "Tate's a real cute little fella."

"He is." She brushed her fingers across his forehead and smoothed back strands of his pale hair. As she moved her hand back to his arm, her fingers trembled. "And truthfully, I'd like him to have a father again."

A father?

The tension he hadn't known was building in his chest suddenly eased, as if someone had loosened a noose that was tightening around him. She wasn't necessarily looking to get a husband. Nope, she wanted a pa for her boy. That was a noble goal, wasn't it? To provide a home and stable life for the little fella?

Maybe they could have a mutually beneficial relationship. By marrying her, he'd get himself out of this embarrassing situation with his family and finally make them happy. And by marrying him, she'd be able to give her son a pa and home.

"Listen," Weston started, but then stopped. What in the blazes was he thinking? He couldn't really be considering going through with such a rash plan, could he? He hardly knew Serena. And she certainly wouldn't agree to it since she hardly knew him.

Yet he was already more acquainted with her than some of the women he'd met through the matrimonial catalogs and newspaper ads. He was also acquainted with her better than some of the random women his sisters and mother had tried to foist upon him. If he'd considered marrying strangers before, why not now?

"Please forgive me. I shouldn't have said anything." She rounded the chair and started toward the door. "If you'll be so kind as to loan me a horse, I'll depart now so that you can spend time with your brother without my interference."

And explain to Maverick that he wasn't really married.

As she passed by, he took hold of her upper arm. "Wait."

Less than a foot from him, she halted but kept her gaze on Tate's sleeping face.

A strange sense of turmoil swirled inside him. It was one he'd experienced with all the women he'd courted, including Felicity. He couldn't explain the feeling, hadn't ever wanted to analyze it. And this time he didn't want to think about it either. He just wanted to shove it away where it couldn't bother him.

He let himself study Tate's face now too. Weston had always wanted children. He wasn't building a successful empire of businesses just for himself. He especially wanted a son who could work with him and who he could pass his holdings along to someday.

"Maybe I can be Tate's pa." He forced the words out before he could think of all the reasons why he shouldn't become the boy's pa.

Serena's gaze rose to his. Her eyes were filled with a dozen questions. Did she doubt his motivation? Think it was too soon?

"As you can see," he continued, "my family is all fired up about me taking a wife. They've been yammering on about it for a while."

"But do you want to take a wife? Especially this soon after having been hurt by Felicity?"

Maybe if his family weren't bothering him so blamed much, he'd wait longer and give himself more time to get over the sting of losing Felicity. But what if marrying Serena helped him put the hurt behind him?

If he didn't marry Serena? He'd eventually have to go through all the hard work of finding another woman and getting to know her. And he was plain tired of the endless cycle of meeting, courting, and rejection.

He could feel the muscles in her arm tensing beneath his touch, so he released her. "I reckon I'm as ready as I'll ever be."

"Are you sure?" Her tone was hesitant, almost as though his hesitancy was making her feel the same.

He'd thought he'd been sure with Felicity, but clearly he'd been wrong. How could a man ever be totally certain? "My pesky family doesn't think I'll ever get married. And I'm aiming to make them eat crow."

"But you don't know me—"

"I know enough for now. And we'll get to know each other better once we're married."

She resituated Tate in her arms, cradling his head against her shoulder. "When would you plan on having the wedding?"

His mind rapidly calculated all the options and then landed on the best one. "Tonight."

Her brow wrinkled again above her nose.

He wasn't convincing her well enough. In fact, she was probably starting to think he was a madman, and at any second she'd run from the house and tell him she never wanted to speak to him again.

He glanced through the doorway into the hall. The voices from the kitchen were still muted, which meant Maverick remained occupied with Maude. "I'd prefer not to lie to my brother or my family. Reckon if we get hitched tonight, then when Maverick trots on home and tells everyone I'm married, that'll be the gospel truth."

She was silent a moment, studying him. "That makes sense. But what if you change your mind in the morning?"

"What if you do?"

She grazed Tate's cheek. Her eyes always contained so much love whenever she looked at the little fella. "I won't change my mind. I need this for Tate."

"And I won't change my mind. I need this for my family."

She wavered again, her expression solemn.

His muscles tensed. "Is there another fella you've set your heart on?"

"No. But Mr. Oakley—Weston?" Her voice dropped to a whisper. "You should know if I do this, it'll be for Tate's well-being. Not for my own. I've been married once already, and I'm not expecting love."

What was she saying? That she had no interest in developing a relationship with him? That she didn't want to have a real marriage? That she was opposed to sharing the marriage bed?

Fact was, he was a single man who'd been waiting a long time for the marriage bed. And Lord in heaven above knew that if he had a wife, he wasn't planning to remain celibate. At least, not for long. Someday soon he'd also be ready to have children.

On the other hand, he'd told her they needed to take some time to get to know each other. Would a few weeks be enough? Maybe by Christmas?

He stuffed his hands into his pockets. "Listen." He cleared his throat. "I'm alright with taking things"—his voice cracked—"well, you know . . . real slow to start with."

Blast. Having this kind of conversation was incredibly awkward. The growing flush in her pale cheeks told him it was awkward for her too.

But it needed to be said so that she knew his expectations.

"Let's wait for—until after Christmas to share—uh, intimacies," he continued. "That oughta give us a heap of time to stop being strangers."

She nodded. "That's very kind of you."

Somehow her words didn't sit quite right with him, but now wasn't the time to analyze them.

"Then a wedding tonight?" he asked softly.

"Alright," she replied just as quietly. "A wedding tonight."

She was almost married again.

Serena stood stiffly beside Weston in the parlor as the pastor, Father Zieber, read the closing remarks from his prayer book. "Those whom God hath joined together, let no man put asunder."

The minister smiled wearily.

Poor fellow. The hour was late—much later than she'd anticipated when she'd agreed to marry Weston tonight.

But Maverick had stayed for a short while after his meal, talking with Weston and catching him up on family news. Even though Serena had joined them in the kitchen, Tate had been awake and hungry, and she'd been busy with him.

She'd heard enough to know that Weston's family had a ranch north of Fairplay, that it was smaller than those in the South Park basin, but that his family had apparently done well enough to make a living from it. From what she gathered, Weston's family was large, and he had more younger brothers and twin sisters.

After Maverick left, Weston had ridden to town to fetch the reverend. Then he'd made a detour to the boardinghouse to let everyone know about the wedding and that she and Tate would no longer be living there. Someone had helped pack her belongings—which hadn't been much, still only one bag. And he'd also located her horse wandering outside the boardinghouse barn.

By the time Weston had returned, the reverend was also just arriving.

Now Maude, standing by the parlor door, was one of their witnesses. And Weston had gone to the cabin out behind the barn and brought with him one of his ranch hands—a middle-aged cowboy with a pock-marked face and one droopy eye, who went by the name Dusty.

Attired in a flannel shirt and wool trousers that reeked of cow flesh, Dusty had positioned himself next to Weston and wore a proud grin, almost as if he were the father of the groom.

Tate leaned against Serena, his hands tangled in her skirt, his grip tight. All of the new people and the new place would be difficult for him as usual. But she prayed that since he liked Weston, he would adjust quickly. He was already fascinated with Ranger. And thankfully the big dog didn't seem to mind Tate's attention, was even now sitting beside Tate almost as though he were a wedding guest too.

Father Zieber continued to read from the order of service in his prayer book. "For as much as Weston and Serena have consented together in holy wedlock and have witnessed the same before God and this company, and have given and pledged their troth either to the other, and have declared the same by giving and receiving a ring . . ." The reverend cocked a brow at Weston.

"Nope." Weston rubbed at the back of his neck as if attempting to ease the tension there. "Don't have a ring yet."

"Do you have anything we can use?"

Weston glanced around the parlor, as if somehow a ring might magically appear. "I'll get a ring tomorrow in town, first thing."

"See that you do." Father Zieber returned his gaze to the prayer book and read silently—likely skipping over the rest of the ring part—then he continued. "I pronounce that they be man and wife together. In the name of the Father, of the Son, and of the Holy Ghost. Amen."

"Amen." Dusty's call rang out cheerfully.

Maude, with her arms crossed, nodded. "Good. Finally."

Weston didn't move, seemed frozen in place. Was he already regretting his decision?

Serena's stomach tightened, her own nerves taunting her. She guessed he was probably feeling the same as she was—wondering if the decision was the right one and praying they hadn't just made a huge mistake.

"Congratulations." Father Zieber snapped the prayer book closed. "I wish you many happy years together."

Dusty clamped a hand against Weston's back. "Oh, don't you worry, Reverend. Weston's gonna be real happy with his new wife. She's a looker. And you know what they say about widows, since they got some experience in—"

"Now, Dusty." The reverend cut in, his voice rising and ending on a squeak. "We're in polite company here." He gave a pointed nod at Serena, then Tate.

Dusty's grin fell away, and he bobbed his head

at Serena. "Sorry, ma'am. Not used to havin' a fine lady such as yourself around and needing to watch what I say. Will try harder, that's for sure."

She offered a smile. "I grew up on a ranch, so I'm not quite as delicate as I appear."

Dusty's smile rose once more, brighter than before. "In that case, I'll be lookin' forward to seeing lots more little ones running around the ranch real soon."

Weston tugged at the bow tie he'd hastily donned before the ceremony, rolling his neck as if he were being strangled.

Serena was uncertain how to respond to such a comment. Saying *thank you* or *me too* seemed slightly inappropriate. But truthfully, she did want to have more children, had hoped Palmer wanted more too. However, since her late husband had been an only child, he'd seemed all too content with just Tate. He'd stopped visiting her bedroom soon after her announcement that she was pregnant, and he hadn't returned after Tate was born.

Even so, she could admit that Weston's plan to get to know each other first seemed to be the wisest course of action. Maybe if they learned more about each other and were able to form a companionable relationship, he might not run off and find pleasure in the arms of another woman the first chance he had.

Whatever the case, she had to be a better wife this time. Yes, she'd married Weston so Tate would have a pa and so that her father-in-law wouldn't be able to take Tate away from her. But what if Weston decided he didn't like her? What if, during the next few weeks until Christmas, he changed his mind—maybe gave her a divorce or an annulment? If he did that, her situation would only look worse. And her father-in-law would have more reasons to accuse her of being an unfit mother.

Father Zieber didn't linger long after the wedding, even though Weston invited him to join them for coffee and dessert. Dusty didn't stay either, winking at Weston on his way out and telling him to have a real good night.

Weston had all but wrangled his bow tie off the moment everyone was gone. Tossing the offending item to the settee, he plunged a hand into his hair, his muscles taut, his jaw clenched tight.

Beside her, Tate continued to cling to her skirt, now staring at Weston with wide eyes. Ranger was still sitting at the boy's side, and the two were nearly the same height. The dog was watching Weston with the same curiosity as the boy, his floppy ears cocking first one way then another, and his eyes shifting with every move Weston made.

Weston blew out a breath. "Reckon I can show you around the house so you can unpack and settle in."

She didn't have much to unpack. Surely he could see that. Regardless, she followed him out of the parlor and tromped behind him up the stairs to the second floor with Tate on her hip and Ranger on her heels.

"The first bedroom is small." Holding up his lantern, Weston pushed open the door to reveal an empty room that was only big enough for a twin bed and perhaps a chest of drawers. "Do you think Tate might like it?"

She stepped in and slowly circled the room. She wasn't a good seamstress, but she could at least make curtains and find a few decorations. It wouldn't be like the spacious nursery at Stony Creek Ranch in Pueblo that had been filled with toys and books, but she could make it cozy and inviting for Tate, couldn't she? "What do you think, Tate? Would you like your own room?"

He lifted his head from her shoulder and peered down at Ranger. "Doggie's room too?"

"No, the doggie already has a bed . . ." She looked to Weston for help. Where did Ranger sleep?

Weston waited in the doorway. "I don't mind if Ranger sleeps in Tate's room."

"Me sleep with Rangie." Tate leaned down low and held out his hand toward the dog.

Ranger lifted his snout, sniffed the boy's fingers, then began to lick them, likely tasting something left there from a meal or snack.

With the dog's tongue tickling him, Tate released a giggle.

At the rare sound, Serena's chest squeezed. When was the last time she'd heard Tate giggle? She couldn't recall. There had been so much tension during their last months at Stony Creek Ranch. Then recently, she'd been so preoccupied with surviving that she'd had little time for small pleasures.

As another of his giggles echoed in the barren room, Serena couldn't hold back a smile.

Weston was watching the interaction between the boy and dog, and a smile quirked at the corners of his lips, softening the strain in his features. "Ranger likes you, Tate."

"I love doggie."

The grip on Serena's chest pinched harder, and heat formed at the backs of her eyes. This place, Weston, the dog—all of it would be good for Tate. Even if the new living arrangement would be strange and challenging for her, it wouldn't matter—not if Tate could finally flourish.

As Weston moved back into the hallway, she trailed after him. He nodded at the closed door across from Tate's room. "Maude sleeps in there."

Weston took several long strides to reach the end of the hallway and a final door. He opened it to a more spacious bedroom.

She approached slowly, not wanting to overstep the boundaries by entering his bedroom, but he motioned her inside as if he thought nothing of her being there.

If it didn't bother him having her in so private a place, then maybe she needed to put aside her own embarrassment.

She sidled past him until she was standing in the middle of the room. It was as sparsely furnished as the rest of the house. A wide bed with a glossy, dark headboard took up one wall and was positioned underneath a large picture window. The cover was neatly pulled up and tucked under the mattress. A tall chest of drawers stood against the opposite wall, and a simple bedside table and chair were the only other furniture. A large stove for heat was positioned in a corner, the wood bin beside it full.

"This is my—our room." Weston had leaned against the doorframe and ducked his head, focusing on Ranger, who was sitting in front of him. "You can unpack your clothing and personal items into the empty drawers, which is most of them. And there's also a closet for you to hang gowns and such."

Gowns? The night she'd run away, she'd only packed the most basic of clothing—her most serviceable dresses and skirts along with her sturdiest shoes. But after wearing the same clothing day after day, she was starting to look shabby. And so was Tate.

However, the condition of their clothing had been—and still was—the least of her concerns.

"Thank you, Weston. You're very kind."

Tate wiggled against her to be let down. She settled him on his two feet, and he bounded over to Ranger and wrapped both arms around the dog.

"Careful now, Tate," she cautioned. "The doggie might not want to be hugged."

The moment she spoke the word *hugged*, Ranger swiped his tongue across Tate's face in a big kiss.

Tate laughed and bent in and kissed the dog's head.

Above the heads of both, Serena caught Weston's gaze. He was smiling again, and she realized that she was too, and that they were sharing the sweetness of this moment together. She'd always longed to share such moments with Palmer, but he'd rarely spent time with Tate, and then only a few minutes at the longest. She guessed Palmer likely would have invested more as Tate got older, would have helped him learn to ride or hunt or fish. But he'd considered the baby stage to be her responsibility.

Weston might too. But at this moment, she liked being able to enjoy Tate's antics with someone else.

Besides, Weston had such a nice smile. It wasn't flashy or overly winsome. Instead, it was simple and straightforward, bringing out the cleft in his chin. It made him more good-looking—if that were possible. Maybe it was the contrast of his smile to the rugged scruff on his face. Or the contrast of his straight white teeth to his tanned skin.

Whatever the case, he was a handsome man. There was no sense in denying that fact.

As though hearing her thoughts and disapproving of them, his smile disappeared. "I'm sorry I only have the one bed for now."

"Me and Mama share bed." Tate's statement came out matter-of-factly. He clearly didn't realize the awkwardness of the predicament, and he released Ranger and ran to the bed as fast as his little legs could carry him.

At the edge, he hefted himself up over the wooden frame, swinging his legs up until he was on the mattress. He scrambled farther onto bed before shifting around and smiling at her. "Look, Mama. Me sleep." He flopped down.

She shook her head and crossed toward him. "No, Tate. This is your new daddy's bed."

As she reached the bed, Tate crawled backward out of her reach. Then he looked at Weston. "Daddy?"

Weston didn't respond. Instead, his eyes widened as if he wasn't sure what to think about being called *Daddy*.

She hadn't discussed with Weston how he wanted to handle Tate. They hadn't really had the time. Did he want Tate to call him *Daddy* or

Pa? Or would he rather the boy address him as Mr. Oakley?

And the bigger problem was, if this was Weston's only bed, where would she and Tate sleep?

Seven

Tate had called him *Daddy*.

Daddy. He'd become a pa.

Weston wasn't sure if that thought should make him happy or scare him. At the moment, he felt a little bit of both.

What did Tate think of having a new pa? From the boy's wide-eyed look, Weston guessed he was trying to figure it all out too.

Serena held out her hands to Tate. "Come to Mama. This isn't your bed."

Tate slowly began to inch toward her. He didn't seem like a willful child, but he definitely didn't want to get off the bed.

Maybe Weston would have to ride to town tomorrow and start tracking down a bed for the boy. Doing so would take some time. In the meantime, with the winterlike temperatures at night, Weston wouldn't even consider rolling out a pallet for Tate on the floor. And he doubted Serena would want the boy to sleep on the settee downstairs.

Of course, Weston could throw down a pallet for himself and give up his bed for the two of them. But that would end up being cold for him too. Besides, it was his house and his bed, and she was his wife. They had every right to sleep near each other.

After all, Serena may as well get used to sharing a room with him, and even the bed, because he was a married man now. Married.

A shimmy of anxiety plied at him. He really was married. Wasn't dreaming.

"I know I said we'd wait and get to know each other . . ." His voice cracked, and he cleared it loudly. "But I reckon it won't hurt nothin' to share the same bed."

Serena kept her focus on Tate. "I understand."

"We can still wait—" He paused and tried to think of chaste words that wouldn't offend Serena or be inappropriate for Tate— "to start having more children."

Tate—and Ranger—were both staring at him again. Weston wasn't a blushing man, not in the least. But he couldn't remember ever having had a more awkward conversation in his life—one that would have made him blush if it were possible.

Serena's cheeks, on the other hand, were turning a shade pinker. "Whatever you want, I'll be fine."

"I promise I won't do nothin' to make you uncomfortable." He wasn't a brute with women. The honest truth was, he'd never forced himself on any woman in the past, and he didn't intend to start now with a wife.

"I'll be fine. Truly." She still didn't look his way.

What was she trying to tell him? That she'd done her duty to her previous husband and would do it with him too?

But was that what he wanted? For her to do her duty? What about a mutually loving and satisfying marriage? Was that possible? Or was that only a dream that few married couples achieved?

"Daddy sleep with me and Mama?" Tate's little voice took on a hopeful note.

Weston shoved away from the doorframe and

began to cross to the bed. As he reached the end, he stood next to Serena. "I'm your pa."

"Pa?"

"Yep. And you can sleep right there, little fella."

Tate nodded. "I be good."

"Of course you'll be good." Weston leaned in and tweaked Tate's nose. "You can sleep in our bed, but only until I get you a bed of your own."

"For me and Rangie?" He held out his hand toward the dog.

Ranger rose from where he'd lain down in the center of the room and sauntered over to the child, his backside wiggling with each shake of his tail. While Tate inched closer to the edge of the bed, Ranger lifted his big black nose and nudged the little boy.

As Serena smiled again at the interaction between the dog and child, the sliver of worry pricking Weston eased just a little. Even if he'd been hasty in making the decision to marry her, and even if he was a little anxious about it, her smiles had a way of soothing him, making him think that he'd done the right thing after all.

"It's late." He turned away from the bed and headed to the stove to add more fuel. "I'll leave you to get ready for bed."

"Thank you." Serena's gratefulness was clear enough. Had she gotten tired of living in the boardinghouse? Or had she really just wanted a pa for Tate? Whatever her motives for accepting the marriage arrangement, he prayed he hadn't made a mistake.

Weston busied himself for the next hour checking on one of the steers with foot rot and another suffering from bloating. When he returned through the back door, Maude wasn't around, and the upstairs was quiet. He turned off his lantern and made his way up the stairway in the dark. He tried to keep his tread soundless, the way Maude was able to do, not wanting to wake up his new family, especially not Tate.

He didn't know much about children, but he reckoned the night would go better if the little fella stayed sound asleep.

Weston slowed even further as he padded down the hallway and entered his room. His pulse stuttered at the realization that never again would he sleep alone. Never again would he be a bachelor. Never again would he come home to an empty house.

Faint moonlight cascaded in through the window above the bed, and it highlighted the two sleeping forms under the thick layers of covers.

They were crowded against the edge of the bed as far as they could possibly go without falling off. Both were facing away from his side, with Serena in the spot closest to him and Tate curled up against her.

He couldn't see either of their faces well in the darkness, but from their silence and the even rhythm of their breathing, he could tell he hadn't disturbed them yet.

He shed his coat, but as he slipped out of his suspenders and let his trousers puddle on the floor, he paused. Maybe he shouldn't get entirely undressed the way he normally did. Maybe he oughta sleep in his clothes instead? He didn't want to scare either Serena or Tate if they woke up to find him in only his undergarments.

On the other hand, they were his family now. They'd have to get used to him being less than proper at times.

As he finished shedding the last of his clothing down to his underdrawers and a light cotton shirt, he flipped back the covers and slipped into the bed.

He situated himself on his pillow, then held his breath, waiting to see if Serena and Tate remained asleep.

At the continued silence from their side of the

bed, he closed his eyes and let himself relax. What was his family gonna say when they heard Maverick's news? He almost smiled thinking about their surprise.

"Weston?" came a soft whisper beside him.

His eyes flew open. As he shifted his gaze to Serena, he found that she was lying on her back and had turned her head so that she was looking directly at him. Her blond-brown hair was loose and free of the constraints of her braid, and her features somehow seemed softer.

He didn't answer her, but he met her gaze. In the darkness, he couldn't see the green of her eyes, but he could feel her scrutiny.

"You've been so kind to Tate," she whispered. "I can't thank you enough."

No one should have to thank a person for being kind to their child. Maybe she and Tate hadn't experienced enough kindness. Maybe that's why they'd come to Fairplay. "You don't have to worry. I'll treat Tate like he's my own."

Her eyes seemed to glisten. Were those tears? "You're a good man."

"I'm just doing what any other man would."

She was quiet for a moment, as though perhaps she was holding back her disagreement. What had her husband been like? She'd said that nothing about him had been particularly easy. Maybe he hadn't been kind to either her or Tate.

"I'll try to be a good wife in return," she whispered.

He shook his head. He didn't want her thinking she had to repay him for anything.

"And I'll try not to bother you—"

"Whoa now." His voice rose, and he quickly dropped it back to a whisper. "You're my wife, and you won't be a bother."

"It's just that this happened so fast, and I don't want you to have regrets."

"I ain't planning on having regrets."

"You're sure?"

He nodded, even though there was still a deep, dark, undefinable place inside that was nagging him. "I have a lot to learn about being a pa and a husband. But I'm a quick learner, and hopefully I won't make too many mistakes."

"It's okay if you do."

"And it's okay if you make mistakes too."

He could see enough of her face to know that he'd made her smile. And for some unexplainable reason, he liked that he'd been able to do that.

She shifted her head and fell silent.

He turned to stare at the ceiling, which was better than staring at her outline. Not that her outline gave him lustful thoughts or anything. But he couldn't keep from thinking on the fact that he had a woman in his bed. A very beautiful woman.

Even so, she was a stranger to him. They'd only met just hours ago—not counting the brief times they'd seen each other around town. There was so much he didn't know about her—so much he probably should've asked before getting married.

But it was too late for that. Come what may, this woman was a part of his life. And now all he could do was make the best of this unexpected marriage.

Eight

"Quiet, Tate." Serena pressed her finger to the little boy's lips as he perched on the bench beside her at the kitchen table. "Your pa is still asleep."

She'd decided to use Weston's term for himself. It wasn't one she'd ever used to address her daddy, but she wanted to do everything she could to make sure Weston loved Tate.

The boy paused in rolling his marble around an obstacle course on the table that she'd made from a few twigs she'd gathered on their way back from the privy. "Pa sleeping?"

"We don't want to awaken him, do we?" The lone lantern at the center of the table cut through the darkness of the predawn hour.

Tate shook his head, his eyes solemn.

"So let's play just as quietly as possible."

Maude was still asleep, too, and Serena didn't want Tate's playing to awaken the housekeeper either.

Tate had always been a light sleeper and early riser. At the boardinghouse she'd simply kept him in their room until she heard noises in the kitchen.

But with Weston asleep in the same bed, she'd hurried Tate from the room at his first waking sound. Thankfully, Weston hadn't stirred, hadn't reached for her, hadn't even accidentally brushed against her. In fact, he'd slept heavily. She should know since she'd hardly dozed throughout the long night.

The truth was—and she'd been too embarrassed to admit it to Weston—her previous husband had never shared a bed with her. After their wedding, Palmer had kept his own room. His infrequent visits in the early months of their marriage hadn't ever lasted long. He'd done what was expected of a husband and then left.

Her marriage to Palmer certainly hadn't been what she'd hoped for. But her daddy had made the arrangements with Mr. Halifax, a longtime friend of his, after Mr. Halifax had written to him about needing a wife for Palmer.

As the second youngest daughter out of ten children, Serena had understood that Daddy was tired of having to make matches for his children and was still grieving over Mother's death. Without Mother's voice of wisdom to guide him, her daddy had sent her west to Pueblo and the Halifax family close to three years ago, when she'd just turned nineteen.

Of course, the Halifaxes were a fine and respected family. They'd offered her a lifestyle similar to what she'd known with her wealthy family. But it had become clear almost from the start that Mrs. Halifax was unhappy with her husband and spent large portions of her day locked away in her bedroom with her laudanum.

At first, Serena had been too naïve to understand Mrs. Halifax's disappointments. But when she'd learned of Palmer's mistress one Sunday at church, she'd finally begun to understand that the Halifax men weren't faithful to their marital vows.

She'd tried to speak of the matter to Palmer, but he'd silenced her with a slap on her cheek. The hit had been hard enough to send the message that she didn't dare talk about the issue again.

Even if her marriage to Palmer had been less than ideal, she'd poured everything she had into being a mother to Tate. She'd loved the little boy as dearly as her own mother had loved her and all her siblings.

But her efforts hadn't been enough, at least for Mr. Halifax. She supposed his grief over losing his Palmer had been difficult to bear. Her decision to take Tate and return to Oklahoma had only added to his sense of loss.

Whatever the reasons, Mr. Halifax had decided that Tate belonged to him more than her, and he'd even told her that she ought to willingly hand Tate over to him to raise now that Palmer was gone, since she was young enough to get remarried and have other children.

But she wasn't ready to give up her son—not to Mr. Halifax, not to anyone.

Tate held out one of the sticks toward Ranger as he rested under the table at their feet. The dog had spent the night sleeping by the bedside and had followed them downstairs when they'd arisen.

Ranger sniffed the stick, then lowered his head back to his outstretched paws.

"Rangie play?" Tate whispered.

"Ranger is still tired." Just like her. She stifled a yawn behind her hand.

"You awake early." Maude's voice came from the doorway.

Serena startled at the housekeeper's unexpected appearance.

The older woman brushed past them to the stove. She was attired in a plain calico skirt and simple matching blouse, but she wore leather moccasins and also a simple beaded necklace.

"I didn't sleep well." Serena pushed up from the bench at the table, wanting to assist Maude in any way she could with the morning chores. While Serena had grown up having servants and had relied on them while living with the Halifaxes, she'd learned a great deal while working at the boardinghouse.

Maude grabbed a handful of kindling. "Weston keep you too busy?"

"Busy?" The moment Serena spoke the word, Maude's implication became all too clear. "Goodness gracious. No." A flush rapidly spread through her. "Not at all."

Maude stood then, abandoning adding fuel to the fire that Serena had already stoked. The old woman narrowed her eyes at Serena, then Tate. "Boy needs his own bed."

At heavy footsteps overhead—Weston's—more mortification pulsed through Serena. She had to put an end to this conversation with Maude before Weston came into the kitchen. She absolutely didn't want him to discover she'd been discussing their bedtime activities—or lack thereof—with his housekeeper.

"Would you like some help getting breakfast ready?" She started toward the large cupboard against the opposite wall. "I can make coffee."

Maude waved a hand impatiently. "No. I do the cooking. You go now. Make Weston happy. That is all."

Make Weston happy?

Serena took a step back from the cupboard. It seemed like such a simple command. But she'd learned from her relationship with Palmer that making her husband happy was one of the hardest jobs.

What could she do to make Weston happy? She didn't know him well enough yet to have learned the things he liked or disliked. Maybe she needed to start a new list with ideas.

She patted her pocket and felt the crinkle of her previous list—the one with the potential husbands. She no longer needed it. But even though she'd accomplished her mission and had a husband, would she be able to keep him?

As Weston's footsteps thudded on the stairway, Ranger crawled out from underneath the table and started to wag his tail. Serena smoothed down her blouse and then her skirt. As she put her hand to her hair, she realized she hadn't yet plaited it.

She ran her fingers through it like a comb. But before she could start a braid, Weston's long stride resounded in the hallway, and in the next instant he filled the doorway. His dark hair was mussed, his shirt unbuttoned, and his stubble thick. He took in first Tate at the table, then Maude adding fuel to the stove, before his gaze landed upon her.

The blue-black of his eyes was filled with questions, almost as if he'd been worried that her absence in the bedroom meant she'd run off during the night. As the taut lines in his face smoothed out, tension also seemed to ease from his shoulders. "You're up early."

His statement was nearly identical to Maude's from a few moments ago. But this time, Serena wouldn't make the same mistake about referencing her sleepless night. "Tate is always up early, and I didn't want him to wake you."

"Don't worry about me." His trousers were low on his hips, one of his suspenders dangling down his leg. As he stretched his arms over his head, his undershirt rose, revealing a span of his stomach—a hard, muscular span tapering into a V that disappeared beneath his trousers.

She'd never witnessed a man so casually attired. Her mother had always been strict regarding the rules of propriety. The Halifaxes had been proper in their conduct and attire as well. Even when Palmer had come to her bed, he'd been covered in his nightclothes and hadn't bared himself in front of her.

This sight now of Weston—she didn't know what to think.

As he lowered his arms and finished a yawn, he stopped short at the sight of her staring at him.

She closed her mouth—which she hadn't realized was open—and spun to face Tate, who was now getting up from his bench.

He clutched the marble in his hand and held it up toward Weston. "Ball, Pa."

She could feel Weston's gaze still upon her and prayed her cheeks weren't turning pink. Maude, in the process of mixing something in a bowl on the opposite side of the table, also halted to stare back and forth between her and Weston.

Serena rapidly began to braid her hair, wishing she'd thought to do it before Weston had awakened.

"Yep." Weston patted Tate on the head at the same time that he thumped Ranger affectionately. "Looks like you've got your ball."

"Mama build roads." Tate returned to the maze of sticks on the table.

Weston approached, still scratching Ranger, the dog thrusting his nose up and giving Weston little choice but to pay him attention.

Tate began to roll the ball through the *roads*. "See."

Weston bent over and followed Tate's movements. "Your ma made the roads?"

Tate nodded.

Weston's profile was rugged, brawn and muscle in every conceivable place. His presence in the kitchen seemed to take up half the room. What was it about him that was so overpowering?

"Looks like your ma is creative." He slid a sideways glance her way, as though he'd felt her staring at him. His dark eyes had a liquid quality—one that was strangely magnetic.

She tore her attention from him and focused instead on Tate, running her fingers through his hair, which hadn't been combed yet either. "I wasn't able to bring any of his toys, so I've had to be creative."

Weston watched Tate for another minute, asking him questions and showing interest in his playing. When he stood, he stretched his arms again and arched his back. That spot of stomach showed once more.

When he patted a hand there, she tore her gaze away only to find him gauging her reaction.

Had he seen her ogling him? This time, she could feel the heat moving into her cheeks. How embarrassing. He was going to think she was a loose woman with the way she was behaving.

She pretended to be preoccupied with finishing her braid, but even the act of braiding seemed too intimate to do in front of Weston, and her fingers fumbled to finish and tie the ribbon.

Maude remained busy in front of the stove, and the scent of both coffee and something cooking began to fill the air. Even as the housekeeper flipped whatever was sizzling in her pan, she was halfway turned, still watching them as if they were putting on a stage production purely for her pleasure.

Weston lowered himself into a chair at the head of the table.

Maude poured a cup of coffee and slapped it

down on the table in front of Weston, the thick sludge-like mixture sloshing over the edge. Then she motioned to Serena and pointed at the spot beside Weston. "Sit."

Serena dropped down and sat unmoving. Tate climbed up on the bench beside her and imitated her motionless posture.

A moment later, Maude plopped another mug of coffee onto the table, this one in front of Serena.

"Thank you," she murmured.

Maude grunted as she moved away.

Weston tapped his thumb against his cup. "How about if we ride into town this morning and do a little shopping?"

She wasn't about to admit to her dire financial situation—that even with what she'd been earning while working at the boardinghouse, she hadn't been able to save much.

Nevertheless, if Weston wanted her to come along to town with him, how could she say no?

"Very well." She hadn't anticipated spending time with him today, had assumed his work would demand his time.

But she wouldn't mind the opportunity to get to know him a little better. In fact, she wouldn't mind it at all.

"Take as much time as you need to shop." Weston veered the team onto a side street on the outskirts of Fairplay.

Tate was wedged between him and Serena on the wagon bench and was holding a portion of the reins Weston had given to him. The little fella had been pretending to guide the team the whole way to town. It was the cutest thing Weston had ever seen.

Even now, Tate was clicking his tongue at the horses the way Weston had.

Weston bit back a smile. Tate was something else.

"I won't need much time," Serena was saying as she held on to her pretty straw hat to keep the breeze from blowing it loose.

"Go and get whatever you need."

"I don't need anything." Serena's statement was quiet, almost embarrassed.

He quirked a brow at her. "What about Tate? Reckon he could use a few new toys."

Tate's green eyes, so much like Serena's, peered up at him. "Toys?"

Serena was shaking her head at the boy in warning.

Weston turned his attention back to the street and the horses and tugged on the reins. "Don't think I've met a better roadbuilder than your ma. But you might find some other toys you like too."

"Me like."

Though the sunshine was warm, the wind gusting from the north brought the reminder that winter was creeping up on them mighty fast.

Serena pulled Tate's cap lower over his ears. "You'll have to be content with what we have for now. Mama is saving for Christmas."

"Your pa is paying for everything today."

"No. Your pa is not paying, because we do not accept charity."

He should've figured that was the issue—that Serena didn't want to be in debt to him for anything. "Your pa is buying Christmas presents today for you and your ma. You can't turn away gifts, can you?"

Tate's eyes widened at the back-and-forth.

Serena shook her head, her lips pursed as she silently tried to communicate with him that she was seeing right through his effort to get Tate on his side.

Did she really think he wasn't gonna be generous and provide for her and Tate? If so, she was about to learn how stubborn he could be when he put his mind to it.

He lifted a hand in greeting to a fellow loitering outside the tenement where many of his mill workers lived. The three-story building contained a dozen apartments. They were dilapidated and hardly livable, but they were cheap.

Lately, every time he visited, he had half a notion to construct his own set of nicer tenements and make them available to his employees. But he already had several other construction projects in various stages and didn't have enough manpower to start more.

As he brought the team to a halt in front of the building, he shifted on the bench so that he was facing Serena squarely. "Listen." He spoke so softly it almost came out a whisper. "You're my wife now, and I'm aiming to take care of you."

"I appreciate that." Her voice was soft too. "But I meant what I said. I don't need anything."

He lifted a brow to challenge her statement.

"Well, maybe a few things. But we're getting by." The bright morning sunshine illuminated her face, turning her skin into soft cream and her eyes into a warm green.

It was clear she didn't know exactly how rich he was. That wasn't a surprise, since he was private with his financial affairs and not many people realized the wealth he was earning from all his ventures in Fairplay and the surrounding towns.

In fact, he could buy her every last item being sold in Fairplay and he wouldn't come close to spending even a fraction of what he'd saved.

"I want to do this for you and Tate," he whispered.

"But—"

"I've been waiting a real long time to take a wife shopping. Let me do it. Alright?"

She seemed to swallow her ready response and instead studied his face.

He liked when she studied him. He'd caught

her doing it a few times earlier and hoped it meant she appreciated what she saw.

At the call of his name from an upstairs window, he waved at Mrs. Shaw hanging half out.

Serena followed his gaze, and a tiny frown formed in her forehead.

He hopped down from the wagon and started toward the front door of the building. "I'm checking on one of my injured workers. Won't be but a minute."

He didn't wait for her response as he ducked past the rickety door into the dank, cold interior lit only by the half-moon window above the door. He took the steps two at a time to the second floor, then he strode down the hallway to the back apartment, where his head saw operator lived with his wife and two young children. The man had nearly lost his arm a couple weeks back when he'd been trying to save one of the other workers from injury. Thankfully, Fairplay had two experienced doctors who had worked together to save Bob's arm.

As Weston knocked and waited, Serena entered below holding Tate on her hip, her eyes widening as though she'd never been in a tenement before.

Her gaze snagged on him, and she started

toward the stairs, apparently having every intention of coming with him. As Mrs. Shaw opened the door, he waited for Serena to reach the landing and join him, made the introductions, then stepped inside the dingy apartment.

He spent a few minutes jawing with Bob about how he was feeling. Same as the last visit, Bob declared he was ready to be back at work in the mill. Weston insisted he recover first, that he'd continue to be compensated for the lost wages.

All the while he spoke with Bob, Serena conversed with Mrs. Shaw and her two children, Tate clinging to her skirt and sucking his thumb.

They stayed longer than he'd anticipated, but once they were back on the wagon bench and heading down Main Street, Serena was full of questions about his employees and their families.

After he parked the wagon near the mercantile and they started toward the store, she paused on the boardwalk, her cheeks flushed and her eyes more alive than he'd seen them yet.

"Do you really want to buy me gifts?"

"Yep. Sure do."

"What will you allow me to get?"

"Anything." At that moment, with how pretty she looked, he'd buy her the world if he could.

"Anything at all?"

"Sweetheart, you can have whatever your heart desires." He liked the idea of being able to spoil her and make her feel mighty special.

A smile worked at the corners of her lips, and he suddenly wanted that smile to be aimed right at him every time.

"Then here's what I'd like." She took a deep breath and lifted her shoulders, as if gaining the courage she needed to state her wish. "Instead of buying anything for myself, could I use the money to purchase Christmas presents for the families who work for you?"

Presents for the families who worked for him? He opened his mouth but couldn't find a suitable response.

She continued before he could gather his thoughts. "I could give them each a gift basket, including some necessary items, maybe baked goods, perhaps even a few toys for their children."

He'd offered her anything. Told her she could get whatever her heart desired. Most women he knew would have enjoyed purchasing new items for themselves and for the barren house.

But Serena? What kind of woman was she to want nothing for herself and instead ask if she could give her portion to strangers?

"I realize this would be a big task." She spoke

earnestly, clutching Tate's hand as the little boy tried to pull her forward. "But my mother did this on occasion for some of the poor families who lived near our ranch. I helped her fill the baskets and deliver them."

It'd be a mighty nice thing to do for all the mill workers and their families. But it'd also be a heap of work, and he didn't want to burden her with all that.

Her eyes shone with expectation.

He couldn't say no and disappoint her. "Let me think on it."

"Thank you, Weston." Her smile spread, bringing a beauty to her features that caught him off guard. In the sunshine, with her lips curved upward and the worry lines gone from her face, she was more than pretty. She was stunning.

He opened the mercantile store door, and she moved inside ahead of him with Tate. Had it been only yesterday that Weston had been jawing with Mr. Dankworth when she'd stepped into the store with the little fella?

"Mrs. Taylor," the store owner called from behind the counter, offering Serena the same smitten smile that he'd given her yesterday. "I didn't expect to see you again today, but what a pleasure." He rounded the counter and shuffled past several barrels, smoothing back his thin hair.

Weston closed the door and stepped directly behind Serena, a strange possessiveness taking hold of him. With the late hour of their wedding last night, the news of their nuptials obviously hadn't spread. He needed Mr. Dankworth and every other single fella in town to know Serena belonged to him now, so that no one got any ideas about stealing her away.

Not that anyone would try it. But with all that had happened so recently with Felicity, he reckoned he was a mite jumpy.

"Mr. Dankworth," Serena said hesitantly, probably wondering how to tell the store owner she was no longer available.

Weston knew exactly how to help her. He closed the last few inches that separated them by pressing his chest into her back and sliding his arms around her waist, embracing her from behind.

At his touch, she drew in a sharp breath but thankfully didn't pull away.

Weston leaned his head down so that his cheek nearly brushed against hers. Was he taking this too far? He hoped he wasn't. He didn't want to scare her away. But at the same time, he needed to show everyone that he had his loop around her. "Serena and me, we got married last night."

Mr. Dankworth halted, as did the other few customers throughout the store, and all eyes turned upon him and Serena and Tate. Mr. Dankworth's expression held more surprise than any of the others.

Weston liked the fella and wasn't fixin' to make him feel bad, but single women in the high country were as rare as a sober man in a saloon. Fair or not, Weston had been the one to win her, although he wasn't exactly sure how.

Her body was soft against his, not even the least stiff, which hopefully meant she wasn't opposed to him putting his hands on her now and again. Course, he wasn't intending to make a regular practice of it yet. Nope, he'd promised her he'd wait for all the touching and kissing and the likes until Christmas, and he was a man of his word.

But today, at this moment, he had to make a statement. "Told Serena she could buy everything in the store if she wants to." Would dangling the possibility of spending a heap of money at the mercantile help smooth over any ruffled feathers?

Mr. Dankworth stared a moment longer, his

smile turning forced. "That's very nice of you, Mr. Oakley. Let me know if I can be of assistance." He sidled back around the counter, his shoulders slumping.

Weston shifted his hold on Serena, suddenly conscious that he'd spread his hands over her waist above her cloak. Even though layers of garments separated his hands from her stomach, he could feel the length of her torso almost all the way to her ribs. She was thin, but she had amazing curves and a womanly figure that were hard not to notice.

Even her backside against him was difficult to ignore. And the scent of her hair and skin. It was a combination of maple, cinnamon, and sugar. He was tempted to dip closer again and take another breath.

But he was making an idiot of himself by standing in the doorway continuing to embrace her. So he dropped his arms away and took a step back. "Ready to shop?"

She glanced around at all the wares, and a small flicker of longing crossed her features before she hid it as she dropped her attention to Tate and fiddled with his hat. "I'd like to wait until you decide on my doing the gift baskets."

Her aspiration was noble, and he liked that

she was so thoughtful and giving and selfless. All the more reason to shower her with gifts. But he was gonna have to do so without her realizing he was giving them to her.

"I've already decided." Really, there wasn't anything to decide.

"You have?"

"Yep. You go on and do them."

"Really?" Her beautiful eyes fixed upon him with genuine gratefulness.

"Only if, in the meantime, you help me start picking out stuff for the house."

"I can do that." She looked around again, this time more eagerly.

He held back a smile. He'd waited a long time for a wife, and he was gonna take full advantage of his ability to spoil her. Every way he could. And maybe, just maybe, this time he'd find true love.

Ten

Serena loved watching Weston teach Tate to ride a horse.

From her perch on the corral fence, she had the perfect place to observe the two—Tate on a gentle old gelding named Sam, and Weston walking alongside, encouraging and instructing him.

"Attaboy." Weston repositioned Tate's hands on the reins. "Now turn Sam my way."

Tate tugged against the reins, his face scrunched with concentration. Old Sam shifted his direction, and Tate broke into a proud grin. "Look, Ma."

Over the past week and a half of living with Weston, Tate had started calling her *Ma* instead of *Mama,* since that's mostly how Weston referred to her. Even though she missed the old name, she could admit she was relieved at just how much Tate adored Weston—enough that he was imitating everything the man did and said.

"I like how you're holding the reins so well." She smiled back at the boy, relishing the late-afternoon sunshine on her face. Even though the day was cold and her breath formed white puffs in the air, the sun made being outside bearable.

Across the corral, Dusty and another ranch hand had sauntered over and now leaned against the split rails to watch the riding lesson. The men who worked the ranch and mills had been accepting of her as Weston's wife and so far treated her respectfully. She could see that they also respected Weston, which didn't surprise her considering how generous and kind he was to them. That had been clear enough during their visit to the Shaws that first day she'd ridden into town with him.

She'd been slightly embarrassed that day at the mercantile when she finally realized that every time she'd suggested something for the house, Weston had immediately added it to his tab— rugs, curtains, vases, candle holders, doilies, framed pictures, decorative pillows, globe lanterns, and more. He hadn't stopped to question any of her suggestions—not even the furniture.

They'd come home with the wagon piled high with all that Weston had purchased not only from Dankworth's but also from Hyndman Bro's and Simpkins.

In addition to assembling the gift baskets for the mill employees, her days had been busy arranging all the new purchases for the house. Slowly she'd begun to transform the place— including Tate's bedroom, which now contained a dresser and night table. Weston was having the bed made by a local carpenter, and for the time being Tate still slept with her in Weston's bed.

In some ways, she was relieved to have the little boy there to distract them. Not that she didn't trust Weston to keep his word about waiting until Christmas to consummate. But somehow, just the act of sharing the bedroom and bed heightened her awareness of him, and she could admit the arrangement was strangely appealing.

Was it because he was so attractive?

Today he was wearing his black Stetson and heavy leather-rimmed trousers with a matching leather coat. The spurs on his scuffed boots jangled with every purposeful step he took. His work-hewn body had the tough look of rawhide but also a rugged swagger of confidence.

Most of the time when she was with him, she just wanted to stare at him. And most of the time she resisted the urge. But right now while he was in his element in the corral with a horse, she couldn't keep from admiring the fine picture he made. Fine, fine picture.

As though hearing her thoughts, Weston shot a glance her way.

She rapidly shifted her attention to Tate with a new Stetson perched on his head—a black one that matched Weston's. He also had new trousers and a thick wool coat. Weston had insisted on buying it all for Tate during the same shopping expedition when they'd picked out the items for the house.

Tate had been thrilled to match his new pa. As if the clothing hadn't been enough, Weston had also purchased almost every toy being sold in the Fairplay stores. Tate had come home with toy horses, play guns, balls of every shape and size, an entire bag of marbles, picture books, a top— more than he'd had in his nursery at Stony Creek Ranch.

When she'd taken Tate over to the

boardinghouse a few days ago to say goodbye to everyone and to thank the Courtney sisters for allowing her to stay there, Tate had been excited to share as much as he could about his new home and toys and clothes. She'd only had to think about the solemn and scared little boy he'd been when she'd arrived to know that she'd done the right thing in escaping from the stresses of living with Palmer's parents.

"You're doing great, Tate," she called.

He flashed his adorable smile again. "Me great."

"Yes, you're catching on fast." Although she could have taught Tate everything he needed to know about horses and riding, she wanted him to have the time with his new pa. Weston was busy most days from before dawn until after dusk. But once he walked into the house after dark, he spent the rest of the evening with them, having supper together and then talking and playing with Tate until the boy's bedtime, which was when she went to bed too.

She supposed at some point she would need to get accustomed to being with Weston alone. But, as with the bed situation, having Tate constantly with her brought a sense of security.

His presence kept at bay any awkward moments with Weston.

For now she was content to allow their marriage to grow slowly. And it was growing. Even with Tate's presence, she and Weston had engaged in many conversations. He'd talked more about his family living in Breckenridge, how hard his pa had worked to build the ranch, the difficulties of their early years living in the mountains, and his parents adopting two of his brothers, Ryder and Tanner, after their pa had died. He'd also told her about his start in Fairplay and all that he'd accomplished.

He'd asked her about her family, and it had been easy to tell him about her parents and siblings and the sprawling cattle ranch she'd grown up on. She'd been surprised at how well he'd listened when she'd talked about how, at seventeen, she'd watched her mother die slowly from pneumonia.

Thankfully he hadn't pressured her to share about her marriage to Palmer, but a part of her worried that perhaps she needed to be more honest with Weston about all that had transpired with her father-in-law after Palmer's death. She wasn't necessarily deceiving Weston. She just hadn't explained her entire situation.

Now that she was married again, hopefully none of it mattered anymore. She prayed that she could finally put that chapter of her life behind her and forget all about her father-in-law's threats.

"How about if we take a little ride?" Weston halted with Tate a few feet from where she sat. His question was directed at her, and his eyes filled with expectation.

She gauged the sun's position above the western range and guessed sunset was at least an hour away.

"I've got something to show you both." Weston's tone had a mysterious and yet excited note to it.

"Me ride." Tate wrapped the reins more securely around his hand.

Weston chuckled. "Not today, little fella. But if your ma says it's okay, you can sit with me and help me with my horse."

Tate's eyes widened. "Ma?"

"Of course."

Weston gave a hand signal to his ranch hands. They grinned at him before ambling toward the barn. As Weston instructed Tate on how to dismount, she climbed down and tugged her cloak around her body, thankful for the heavy garment and the hood.

A moment later, Dusty reappeared leading Belle and Weston's gelding. With both horses already saddled, it was clear Weston had been planning the outing, and she couldn't keep from being just a little thrilled at his efforts.

In no time they were riding across the narrow bridge that spanned the South Platte River. Weston led the way into the foothills for a short while, reining in as they reached the edge of a thicket of blue spruce.

"Here we are." Weston swung his leg over his saddle and slid down effortlessly, surveying the pines.

The hills cast long dark shadows over the trees and brought the chill of the cloudless evening. But the sunlight was still cascading over the distant snow-covered peaks.

Weston hefted Tate down, and Serena dismounted at the same time. Then Weston flipped open his saddle bag and removed an axe. As he slung it over his shoulder, he nodded to the evergreens, their boughs thick and the air laden with their scent. "Since we have less than two weeks until Christmas, reckon we need to get us a Christmas tree."

Tate peered at the nearest tree, one that had only half its branches. "Kiss-mas tree?"

"Yep."

Since Tate was only two, he likely didn't remember Christmas the previous year. Even though Mrs. Halifax hadn't thought to decorate for Christmas, Serena had done the best she could to add some festivity to the home. But finding and cutting a tree had been out of the realm of her abilities.

Serena reached for Tate's gloved hand, clasping it in hers. "A Christmas tree is a special tree that we bring into our home at Christmas time. We'll decorate it with all kinds of ornaments—strings of popcorn, buttons, and dried fruit. Then we'll also make ornaments from paper and candy."

"Me decorate Kiss-mas tree?"

"Oh yes. You and me and your pa." She glanced to Weston, hoping she wasn't overstepping herself by including him in the decorating.

He nodded. "As soon as you and your ma have the decorations ready, then we'll do it together."

Tate hopped up and down, his face alight with excitement.

For a short while they meandered through the trees, searching for the right one. She soon found herself laughing with Weston over Tate's antics, as he seemed drawn to the most deformed and disfigured of trees, especially those missing pine needles. Or he picked out impossibly tall trees or those too small to decorate.

Finally, they managed to find the right tree. Weston made short work of chopping it, then he tied it to the saddle behind him, and they reached home just as the sun was beginning to set. As Weston carried the tree inside, Tate held on to a branch, hefting and hauling the same way Weston did.

A small piece of Serena's heart ached at the picture of her son imitating the strong cowboy. It was almost as if she was grieving for all that she'd never had with Palmer. Even if Palmer hadn't died in the brawl, she couldn't picture him suggesting going to get a Christmas tree, much less bringing it inside and setting it up. He'd never been interested in the doings at home, had always spent his free time in town or visiting with friends. Weston, on the other hand, genuinely seemed to relish every moment of their time together.

After Weston nailed two boards to the bottom

of the tree to form a stand, he positioned it in the corner of the parlor.

"It's beautiful." She'd shed her cloak and had helped Tate from his. The warmth from the fireplace was beginning to thaw her fingers and toes, but her nose and cheeks still tingled from the ride. Now she held Tate's hand to keep him from interfering with Weston's efforts.

Thankfully, Tate had waited patiently for Weston to complete the base, and he watched with rounded eyes, taking in the spruce tree that looked absolutely perfect even without any trimmings.

Weston stepped back until he was standing beside her. He was close enough that his arm brushed against hers. His coat was discarded with theirs, and he'd rolled up his sleeves, revealing the muscular tendons and prominent veins that ran up and down his arms.

He was a strong man. Not only physically, but he exuded an inward strength as well—one that wasn't overpowering or demanding or arrogant but steady and dependable and humble.

She could feel him giving her a sidelong glance, so she shifted enough to meet his gaze. "Thank you for this and for everything."

"You're welcome." His eyes were especially

dark, almost like midnight. Intense and probing. Was he searching her? If so, what did he want to see?

She shifted her attention back to the tree, suddenly breathless.

His hand brushed hers.

She didn't move. Was it accidental?

His fingers touched hers again, this time his pinky caressing the length of her pinky.

Her heart picked up its pace. That was most definitely not an accident. So what did it mean?

As he made another trail, he hooked his pinky through hers. Then he simply stood there, his pinky linked with hers as they stared straight ahead at the tree.

She could hardly focus. All she could think about was this slight connection she was having with him. It was sweet and tentative, almost as though he wasn't quite sure what he really wanted yet from their marriage.

She'd been trying not to think about the fact that he hadn't yet given her a ring—even though he'd told Father Zieber he would get one for her right away. But at this hesitant touch, she could sense that perhaps he was fighting fears of his own.

Was it possible they could both fight their

battles together? And come out stronger as a result?

Before she could decide how to approach the question, he slipped his hand away from hers, breaking their contact. He pivoted away, swiped up his coat from the back of the chair where he'd draped it, then stalked across the room.

"I need to finish some chores. I'll be back for dinner." Without another glance back, he exited the parlor. A moment later, the front door closed behind him.

She exhaled a shaky breath. She'd never been in love before—never even had feelings for a man, not even Palmer. So whatever this was she was beginning to feel for Weston was new, strange, even a little frightening.

Maybe it was for the best if she squelched it now while she still could, before it got too big. Although she feared that maybe she was already too late.

Eleven

"It's just around the next bend." Weston glanced behind him to make sure Serena was still on his trail.

Serena and Tate were draped in a bearskin robe atop Belle and plodded steadily along only a few paces away, the snow having given way to damp leaves and soil now that they were in the open Blue River Valley.

He breathed out a puff of relief that the trip hadn't been as difficult as he'd anticipated. Serena's faithful horse had handled the snow-covered trail and Hoosier Pass just as well as she'd predicted. Even though the distance between his home and his family's ranch was only twenty-two miles, the hard trek over the pass added extra time. On a good day he could cover the distance in three hours. They'd made the journey in a little over four.

"You're a good rider," he said over his shoulder.

"You sound surprised."

"Reckon I shouldn't be, not with you having grown up on a ranch."

"I can ride better than a lot of men."

"Blamed right."

His offhand compliment earned a half smile from her.

He slowed his mount and fell into step beside her. Engulfed in the thick dark fur, she looked like a pale fairy princess. Even though she had a rosy nose and cheeks, she'd assured him every time he'd asked that she was fine. Tate seemed warm enough too and had fallen asleep in spite of the jarring ride.

Weston let himself feast upon Ten Mile Range to the west with its snowy slopes and white peaks and miles upon miles of mountains running from north to south. The sight was as majestic as it had always been from the moment he'd first stepped into the area.

The higher elevation was a rugged and often difficult environment, even more so than Fairplay, and had helped shape him into the man he was. He was thankful for that. Yet he was glad he'd made his own way. As much as he loved his family, his ambitions had always soared beyond his pa's. He'd always been more driven, his plans bigger, his goals higher.

There hadn't been enough in Breckenridge to keep him there eight years ago. Not after losing Electra. But over recent years, as the settlement had grown and more people had moved to the area, he'd begun to see the potential for buying land and developing it.

He was even considering the option of building another mill since the Blue River flowed through the valley. While he was visiting his family for the next few days over Christmas, he wouldn't pass up the opportunity to investigate land options.

For now though, he needed to prepare Serena for meeting his big and overbearing family.

With Christmas only two days away, it was hard to believe he'd been married for about three weeks. Parts of the three weeks had gone faster than a greenie flying from a greased saddle. He'd helped decorate the Christmas tree so that it had been real pretty. When Serena had finished putting together the gift baskets, he'd joined her in delivering them, much to the surprise and delight of each of his employees.

Course, he'd kept up the riding lessons with Tate as often as he could—a couple times a week. And he'd gone shopping with Serena again, this time so that he could get her help buying for his family. Now his saddlebags were full with all that he'd purchased.

Yep. He and Serena had fallen into a real nice routine together. She was easy to talk to and be with, and so was Tate. Their presence in the home—and all her work at fixing it up—had been everything he'd ever dreamed of having in a wife and child.

But . . . parts of the three weeks had gone slower than a cow crawling through a cactus patch. Especially those parts where he'd been in the same bed with her. Like every night.

It'd been a good thing she kept the same bedtime routine as Tate and was already asleep whenever he lay down so that he wasn't tempted to reach for her. It was a good thing he was a heavy sleeper so that he didn't accidentally pull her into his arms while he slept. And it was a good thing she got up every morning before he did and was well out of the room before he could drag her back down when she was all sleepy-eyed and flushed.

Somehow he'd managed to make it through the nights. And maybe it was for the best Tate's bed wouldn't be finished until the day after Christmas. Because having the little fella sleeping only inches away had also squelched the temptation to draw Serena close.

He could admit he was still afraid things were too good to be true. It'd been that way with every woman he'd courted. He'd thought he was making progress, thought he was winning her over, thought things would work out, but in the end everything always fell apart.

Whatever the case, the getting-to-know-each-other phase with Serena was fast coming to an end. Was it time to finally put his fears to rest and stop holding himself back?

He stuck his gloved hand into his coat pocket, and his fingers connected with the square box containing the ring he'd purchased the day after their hasty wedding. He hadn't given it to her yet. He'd been waiting for the right moment, but one hadn't come along—at least, not one that had felt right.

"This sure is different than Oklahoma." Her voice held a note of awe as she surveyed the mountains on both sides of the river valley.

"And different than Pueblo?" he asked.

She hesitated. Except for the brief comments she'd made on their wedding day, she hadn't spoken again about her first husband. She hadn't even talked about Pueblo and the ranch there. The honest truth was, he wanted to hear what her experiences had been like. Had her husband loved her? Had he loved Tate?

Weston couldn't imagine anyone not loving either of them.

Loving. His grip tightened on his reins. It was too soon to be falling in love with Serena. Wasn't it? He'd figured with their marriage being one of convenience—a mutually beneficial arrangement for both of them—that it might take a while for them to learn to love each other.

But the fact was, she was an amazing woman. He couldn't remember ever meeting another woman as giving, generous, and considerate. And she was an excellent ma to Tate, always loving but firm when needed.

Even Maude liked Serena—and that was a feat, since Maude didn't like too many people.

He drew in a breath of the thin but crisp

high-altitude air and watched as the first sight of the ranch came into view: the split-rail fencing that ran the length of the wide-open grassland. At the center of the long stretch of fence, smooth log beams formed an entrance surrounding the wide metal gate. The top log was emblazoned with black metal letters that spelled out the name: *High Country Ranch.*

A dirt road wound back for at least a quarter of a mile before reaching the main house, which was situated at the base of a slope.

"There." He pointed to the wisp of smoke rising from a large log house, barely visible among the pines that surrounded it and provided a buffer against the snow and cold.

Serena straightened and followed his gaze to the house then looked north to the barns and corrals near several other smaller cabins for the hired men.

During this time of year, the main herd of cattle grazed in the enclosed fields around the ranch. But during the summer and autumn months, the cattle had free range to wander into the gulches and higher grassy pastures.

Mostly, though, his family bred horses. With the influx of settlers since Colorado had become a state, the need for horses had swelled. His pa and younger brothers were making a decent profit as they attempted to keep up with the demand.

Weston nodded toward the south field closest to them and the dozens of horses grazing there— the bays, chestnuts, blacks, grays, and roans. "My pa has invested more in horses over recent years."

She studied the herd. "Looks as though he has Morgans and mustangs?"

"A few Percherons and Clydesdales too."

"Some Appaloosas?" She nodded toward the group of spotted horses grazing together.

"Nope. Actually, those are a new breed my pa's been developing—one he's calling Colorado Oakley."

"They look tall and tough."

"Yep, they're bred to be steer savvy and hard workers."

They were approaching the gate, and he slowed his mount. As soon as his family converged, he likely wouldn't get any more time alone with Serena until they started back to Fairplay in a few days. He could admit he'd enjoyed the extended time with her over the past hours of traveling, and he wasn't ready for it to end.

"Reckon I oughta warn you about my family." He reined in at the ranch entrance.

She halted beside him. "That sounds ominous."

He peered down the dirt road but didn't see anyone. His pa and brothers and the other ranch hands were probably hard at work on one project or another at a remote part of the property or busy in the barns. The work on a ranch was never-ending, which was why he'd kept his spread in Fairplay small, so that he had the flexibility to pursue other ventures.

"No doubt about it, I love my family." He slid down from his mount. "But they're loud and busy. And they let you know what they think, whether you want them to or not."

"As they did with you about a wife?"

He slipped open the gate latch. "Yep. They've been nagging me worse than horseflies."

"I'm honestly surprised you didn't have a wife yet with as kind and good-looking—" She halted and then gave her head a curt shake as if admonishing herself. "I mean kind and generous."

As he swung the gate wide, he couldn't keep a grin from kicking up his lips. "So you think I'm good-looking?"

"Of course you are." She dipped her head, avoiding his gaze. Were her cheeks getting rosier?

"It's a plain fact, and I'd be lying if I told you otherwise."

"Well, you're mighty fine yourself." She was more than *fine*. Even more than *mighty fine*. Especially sitting atop her black mare, wrapped in the bearskin, with the white peaks forming a backdrop behind her.

She kept her focus on Tate, whose long lashes rested against his cheeks.

What would it hurt to tell Serena some of how he was feeling about her? He might as well give her the compliment he'd been wanting to since they started out of Fairplay. "The honest truth is, you're so beautiful that I'd rather look at you than anything else."

Okay, so maybe that was too much sharing. He could have tamped down his ardor just a pinch instead of blathering like a besotted boy.

"That can't be the truth," she responded softly, peering out over the landscape again. "Nothing can compare to this."

"You can." There he was, doing it again. Making a fool of himself.

Though she didn't smile, her eyes filled with gratitude. "Thank you, Weston. You've been kinder to me and Tate than we deserve."

"This ain't about kindness, sweetheart. This is

about the truth." Maybe his tongue was looser after the hours he'd just spent with her. Or maybe it was just getting harder to ignore his growing attraction. Whatever the case, his words were getting away from him today.

Thankfully, Tate chose that moment to open his eyes and sit up. As Weston climbed back on his horse and they started down the lane, he couldn't keep from stealing more glances at her, unable to stop himself from admiring her.

As they passed through the woodland of towering lodgepole pine, the house came into view, festive with boughs and wreaths decorating doors and windows. Before they could dismount, the front door swung open, and his ma stepped out onto the spacious raised porch.

Wiping her hands on her apron, she beamed as though she'd won a fortune in gold. Her face retained a youthfulness that belied the all-gray bun piled loosely on her head—gray that had come early. He didn't remember exactly when her hair had stopped being blond-red, but he suspected the change had happened when Pa had been fighting in the war and life had been especially stressful.

"Weston Charles Oakley," she called even as her gaze settled upon Serena and Tate. "I heard you were married, but I told Mav I wouldn't believe it until I saw it."

"Yep, Ma. I'm married." Thank the good Lord for that. He wasn't sure he could've survived one more visit with all the pestering.

Before Ma could get another word out, Clementine and Clarabelle were stepping onto the porch, drying their hands on their aprons too. As slender as Ma, the two were nineteen and nearly identical in their looks, having wavy blond hair with hints of red, bright green eyes, and naturally pretty features.

"I still don't believe it." Clementine flashed her sassy smile. "I predict Wes bribed the woman to pose as his wife."

"Clementine." Ma leveled a stern frown upon the girl.

"What?" Clementine pretended false innocence. "I'm simply repeating what Pa said."

Weston didn't dare meet Serena's eyes and chance giving away the truth—that they were almost correct. The marriage had been a bribe of sorts.

"You're being rude." Clarabelle, the quieter and more reserved of the twins, could still match Clementine with the amount of trouble she could cause. But thankfully, today she seemed inclined to be polite. She gave Serena a welcoming smile. "We're so glad you're here. Thank you for finally getting Wes to commit when no other woman could."

Weston sighed. One thing was for certain with his family: he never knew exactly what to expect.

Twelve

S erena awakened to a strange sense of contentment. She blinked in the early morning light and tried to gain her bearings in the loft where she, Tate, and Weston had been sleeping at his family's home

The memories came rushing back of the past two days at High Country Ranch with Weston's family. He'd been right to warn her. His family was loud and busy and always getting involved in each other's lives.

But after the initial introductions, the Oakleys had easily accepted her and Tate, welcoming them in as if they belonged. In fact, Weston's mother, Hannah, had gushed over Tate so much that the little boy had taken to her faster than he ever had to anyone else.

"He's my first grandchild," Hannah had declared with one of her warm smiles. "Of course I'm gonna spoil him."

Tate had not only become enamored with his new grandma but with his aunts too. Although it had taken him longer to trust Clementine and Clarabelle, by last evening he'd been sitting on their laps, letting them hug and kiss him and read him stories by the firelight.

The time with Weston's family had gone by quickly, mostly filled with cooking and eating and talking. But they'd also taken a sleigh ride around the ranch, gone sledding on nearby foothills, and attended a Christmas Eve service last evening at the church in Breckenridge.

She'd enjoyed spending time with Weston's family, including not only Maverick but Weston's other adopted brothers—Ryder and Tanner. Weston's pa was quieter and more reflective than the others, but he exuded a strength and wisdom that everyone respected.

Serena turned in the bed and reached for Tate to draw him closer. Feeling the empty spot beside her, wakefulness rushed in, and her pulse picked up speed. Where was he? Had he wandered off somewhere?

At his giggle coming from the living quarters right beneath the loft area, her heart rate slowed. Of course he was safe. Hannah had probably tiptoed up to the loft and carried him down just as she had yesterday morning when she'd heard him stirring. Except yesterday Serena had already been awake and trying to keep Tate from talking and waking Weston.

Clearly, without Tate in bed wiggling around, poking her eyes, or patting her cheek, she'd been able to sleep later this morning. How long had it been since she'd had that luxury?

She stretched languidly, but her bare foot brushed against another foot. Weston's. She held herself motionless.

His breathing remained even and heavy, as it always was when he was sleeping.

They'd had accidental contact under the covers over the past month, but thank goodness, the brief touches had never woken him.

She started to inch her foot away from his, but before she could move, he rolled from his back to his side, draping his arm across her waist.

She froze. What was he doing?

Once again she listened to his breathing. It

remained unchanged. She turned her head enough that she could see his face. From the glow of a lantern and the fireplace down in the front room, enough light filtered up that she could see his features.

The layer of scruff on his jaw was darker and thicker than usual. His hair was endearingly messy, strands begging her to run her fingers through them and brush them back. And his normally taut muscles were relaxed, as if all the worries of his life had disappeared for just a few hours.

She rotated a little more, the chill of the loft skimming her nose and cheeks, but underneath the layer of thick blankets, her body was plenty warm, especially with Weston's heat against her.

She'd never thought she'd get accustomed to sharing a bed with a man, had assumed it would be as awkward and unpleasant as Palmer's visits had always been. But after the first few nights of worrying next to Weston, she'd realized she had nothing to fear from him. In fact, the sharing of their bed had become strangely companionable. His strength and power beside her was actually comforting.

Did she dare admit she liked this man who was now her husband?

His arm lay heavily over her, but it didn't feel suffocating or disagreeable. In fact, his touch was even somewhat exciting.

His hold was warm and solid . . . and caring. Weston cared about her. And that's what made him different from Palmer. Her first husband had never cared about her, hadn't even taken the time to get to know her. They'd been strangers when they married, and they'd remained strangers until he died.

But Weston . . . Since the first day, he'd shown her in large and small ways that he valued her and Tate—the shopping trips, the horse-riding lessons, the Christmas tree expedition. Even while here at his family's home, he'd made sure she was included, had everything she needed, and was enjoying herself. Sure, he'd gone off with his pa and brothers often to talk and work. But even when he was gone, she'd known he'd be there for her if she needed anything at all.

She let herself take in his broad chest, his undershirt stretching taut from shoulder to shoulder. She hadn't been exaggerating that day when she'd called him good-looking. Maybe she hadn't meant to tell him, but it had been the truth.

You're so beautiful that I'd rather look at you than anything else.

His reverent words had played over in her mind dozens of times since he'd spoken them before their arrival at the ranch. Even now the compliment swelled within, adding warmth to her body.

"Merry Christmas." His gravelly whisper startled her.

Her gaze flew to his face to find that his eyes were half open. And oh, goodness gracious, with his head on his pillow, he looked even more appealing than he did when he was all rugged cowboy.

"Merry Christmas," she whispered back. She had a little gift for him, something she'd managed to purchase with the meager earnings she had left from working at the boardinghouse. Should she give it to him now in private? It wasn't much, but hopefully he'd realize it expressed her gratitude to him for all he'd done for her.

His eyes opened a fraction wider, taking in the empty spot next to her. "Where's Tate?"

"Your mother must have come for him." She paused and listened. Tate's voice still mingled with Hannah's in the room below.

Weston seemed to also listen for a moment

too before his lips curved into a gentle smile. "She's in heaven to finally have a grandbaby to love." He shifted his arm that was across her, then startled as he took in his position.

"Darn it all," he whispered as he started to lift his arm away. "Didn't mean to—"

Her hand darted out before she could think through her actions, and she captured his hand and brought it back down on her waist.

He grew entirely motionless, didn't even seem to be breathing.

Instead of immediately releasing him, she held on for an extra second. Then before she could make herself let go, she shifted his hand so that it was flat on her stomach.

Slowly he fanned his fingers out, spanning most of her abdomen and covering part of her ribs.

The heat of his touch seared through her nightgown so that she almost felt as if there were nothing between them. With her hand still upon his, she couldn't move, couldn't breathe, couldn't think of anything but the intimacy of his hold.

He seemed to start breathing again, but raggedly.

She waited, her muscles tensing for what he

might do next. Would he do something else? Now that she'd given him permission to touch her?

Did she want him to caress her elsewhere? Was she really ready for that next step in their relationship?

He shifted his head on his pillow, his uneven breathing now closer to her ear.

She closed her eyes, bracing herself, unsure of what was happening but wanting more, maybe even *needing* more from him.

The warmth of his exhalations filled her ear, echoing so that suddenly her whole body seemed to awaken to him and the realization that his long, hard body was nearly brushing against her.

The awareness of him left her almost breathless, and she waited again—for what, she didn't know. Him to press a kiss on her ear? Into her hair? Maybe lean his body against hers more fully?

He didn't move for an agonizing few seconds, then he dropped his head lower so that his breathing now caressed her neck.

Would he kiss her? Oh yes, she wanted him to. She couldn't deny it.

Her fingers, still over the top of his hand on her stomach, tightened with need.

In turn, his hand beneath hers widened, his

muscles growing taut. In the next moment, his lips touched her neck.

She couldn't hold back a soft gasp—one of both pleasure and surprise. She supposed it had been loud enough that anyone listening in the room below might have heard her. But with Weston's lips upon her neck, she couldn't find the decorum to care.

His mouth was tantalizing—so much so that she nearly arched up, need rising within her. Need she didn't understand but that she wanted to explore with him.

He laid first one kiss and then another on her neck, making a trail toward her collarbone, following her pulse. With each kiss, she gasped again, then again. Each barely audible, but distinct enough to draw Weston closer so that, before she realized it, he was flush against her side.

As his mouth finally closed over her collar bone, she arched into his hand on her stomach. She couldn't hold back a murmur of pleasure and might have even released a strangled cry, but then Tate called out from the steps. "Ma? Pa? Me open presents?"

The call sliced through Serena's haze of wanting. She scrambled up and away from

Weston, attempting to put as much distance between them as possible before Tate arrived, no doubt with Hannah on his heels.

Sure enough, a second later Tate's blond head appeared on the steps, with Hannah right behind, keeping a steady hand on his back to prevent him from toppling down the stairs.

Hannah's smile was smug as she helped heft the boy up the last steps. "He heard your hanky-panky and came to investigate, even though I tried to distract him to give you a little more time."

Tate climbed to his feet and then came running toward the bed as fast as his little legs would allow. "Me presents?" His face was filled with such expectation, and his eyes were rounded with wonder.

"He's ready for Christmas." Hannah stared at Serena and Weston and made no effort to hide her curiosity. "Too excited to wait for his ma and pa to—"

"Okay, Ma," Weston cut in. He reclined against his pillow, one arm propped behind his head, looking as calm as if he were talking about the weather. But oh so handsome, his biceps straining, his body stretched out, his legs crossed casually.

Tate crawled up onto the bed and plopped down between her and Weston.

"You ready, little fella?" Weston tousled Tate's hair.

Tate nodded vigorously. "Me ready."

Serena couldn't get her voice or thoughts to work like they normally did. Instead, she made the mistake of looking at Weston's mouth. At those lips that were just seconds ago taking their sweet time kissing her neck—lips that she wanted upon her neck again.

Could she find an excuse to send Tate back down with Hannah? Maybe Hannah could feed him his breakfast?

Hannah's smile moved into her eyes and crinkled the corners. "I just love seeing you two acting like newlyweds, and I'm sorry you couldn't have more time alone this morning."

"It's alright." Weston's tone took on a note of embarrassment.

"Sheesh, it's Christmas morning," someone called from downstairs. Was it Maverick? "You can finish up later when we're not all waiting for you."

Oh no. Serena's heartbeat crashed to a halt.

"Let them at least have a last good morning

kiss," came another call—a woman's voice. Clementine?

Had the entire family been awake when Weston started kissing her? Maybe the hour was later than she'd realized. Or maybe they'd all heard Tate and had awoken early to be with him.

Whatever the case, the family was congregated downstairs.

Serena could feel the heat of mortification moving into her cheeks.

"That's a good idea," Hannah was saying to Weston. "Give your wife another kiss and then come on down."

"Nope, we're fine." Weston's response was quick.

"Go on and give her a kiss, Wes." This call came from his pa. "We can wait a minute."

"Or five." Another voice dripped with humor. Was that Ryder? Or Tanner?

Goodness gracious. The whole family *was* downstairs waiting. And Weston had been entirely right about them all interfering in each other's affairs. In fact, they took interference to a new level.

Serena pressed her cold hands to her cheeks.

"You're not getting out of it, Wes." Hannah

chuckled. "Give Serena a final kiss. I could tell she wanted more."

Could this moment get any more embarrassing? Serena sank back into the mattress.

Before she could grab her pillow and bury her burning face into it, Weston bent closer. He hovered above her, his eyes apologetic.

Tate, who had moved near their feet, was staring between her and Weston as if waiting.

Since it appeared that she and Weston were destined to kiss again in the bed this morning, she'd have to keep it short and sweet with Tate looking on.

"They kiss yet?" The question rose to the loft.

Weston leaned in even farther, his chest brushing hers. Somehow, just that tiny contact took her back to a few moments ago when he was kissing her neck. The delicious heat returned but this time in a rolling wave that rippled through her.

He brought his hand up to her face, his fingers soft as he grazed her skin and then cupped her cheek. He focused entirely on her mouth, as if it were the prize and he wanted it more than he wanted anything else.

Her breath hitched, her chest rising against

his and feeling the weight of him pressing in. She had the undeniable urge to wrap her arms around him and hold him close and never let go. But before she could manage to slip her hands around to his back, his mouth descended upon hers.

She wasn't sure what she'd been expecting. Perhaps the hard and unrelenting tension that had resulted when kissing Palmer. Never tender. Never passionate. It had almost been angry.

But with Weston, his mouth covered hers tenderly, as though he didn't want to push her too far, as though he intended to keep the kiss light and short, as though he was afraid he'd crush her.

But she wasn't crushable. She'd had to prove that many times over the past years—with her mother's death, with Palmer's unfaithfulness, with her father-in-law's accusations. She was a strong woman. And she wanted a strong kiss.

Without caring who was watching and listening and waiting, she reached for Weston's neck just as he began to back away. She wrapped her hands behind him and held him in place. In the same moment, she tilted up and chased after his lips.

He paused, clearly uncertain and unprepared for her initiating more.

She glided her fingers through the hair at the back of his neck and at the same time stroked his lips, asking him, urging him for more.

He hesitated just a moment longer, then dove back into her with a soft groan. This time he didn't hold back. Instead, the pressure was certain and hungry, as if she'd offered him a delectable dessert and he planned to have every morsel.

She wanted to have every single taste of him too. He was delicious—more delicious than anything she'd ever tried before.

His kiss turned hard and deep, each needy surge faster than the last, as if he was trying to get as much as he could before the feast was taken away. For a reason she didn't understand, his need only seemed to make her hungrier for more.

Little hands upon her legs tugged at her. Tate.

Tate was watching them kiss. Oh, lunacy of lunacies.

She broke away from Weston and scrambled off the bed. She stood as much as the slanted ceiling would allow, her breath coming in bursts, her chest heaving, her body trembling.

With her hands against her cheeks, she didn't dare look at Weston. She was too embarrassed to meet Hannah's gaze. Instead, she reached for wide-eyed Tate and hefted him onto her hip.

"Are you ready for Christmas?" Her voice came out shaky.

He nodded.

"Me too." She'd married Weston to keep Tate safe, hadn't thought about herself or what she wanted from a marriage or really even in life. But here with Weston and his big, endearing family, she wanted everything she'd thought she'd lost and would never have again—love, happiness, and the promise of a future.

Hannah had already started back down the stairs. And the murmur of voices from below told her that the rest of the family had been satisfied with their kiss and were moving on to other things.

But Weston? He'd draped his eyes with the crook of his arm and lay silent, unmoving in the bed. What was he thinking?

A moment later, he rolled over and climbed off the other side of the bed. As he stood, he swiped up his trousers from the floor and rapidly stuffed first one leg, then the other in them. With his back facing her, she couldn't see his expression or measure his reaction to all that had just transpired.

As he reached for his shirt, he started toward the stairs, slipping an arm into one sleeve as he walked. His back was rigid and his jawline taut, almost as if he was upset.

He paused on the top step as he drew up his suspenders. "Take your time. I'll meet you downstairs." He spoke quietly, almost tersely, and then continued without waiting for her response.

Had she done something wrong? Maybe she'd been too forward with the kiss. She opened her mouth to apologize but then stopped herself. She'd offered him her love. And there was nothing wrong with that.

Her love. Was it possible she was already falling in love with Weston?

Her heart swelled, longing mixing with fear. Yes, it had been easy to fall for a man as wonderful as Weston. But what if he wasn't ready to love her in return? What if he decided she wasn't enough for him? Especially when he learned more about her past?

She should have been honest with him from the start about the true reason she'd married him—to avoid losing Tate to Palmer's family. And she should have confessed that she'd planned their chance meeting that day on the road to his house.

She had to tell him—she would tell him . . . Maybe on the long journey back to Fairplay tomorrow.

In the meantime, she'd keep trying to win his fondness. And she'd pray that this time, with this marriage, she could finally be enough.

Thirteen

Serena couldn't remember ever having a Christmas celebration as festive as the one she was sharing with the Oakleys.

Even if the kisses with Weston had been an unexpected way to start the day, his family had teased them for only a minute or two before Tate's excitement over the opening of gifts had distracted everyone.

She lifted the coffee pot from the back burner and began to refill Weston's cup. The laughter and conversations in the front room wafted even to the far corners of the kitchen. The morning sunshine bathed the room, warming her. And the scents of cinnamon and sugar lingered in the air from the sweet rolls one of the twins had made and served while they'd been opening the gifts.

"I thought I saw you sneaking off." Hannah's cheerful voice came from behind Serena.

"Weston's coffee was low." Serena finished pouring the cup.

Hannah stood at the table and was sliding another sweet roll onto her plate from the few left in the pan. "He shouldn't be asking you to do that for him, dear. He's capable of refilling his own coffee."

"He didn't ask me." Serena set the cup on the table and reached for the small pitcher of cream. "I wanted to do it for him to be a good wife."

Hannah wiped her sticky fingers on the apron that covered the red calico dress she'd donned for the holiday. With flushed cheeks and sparkling eyes, the matron looked as though she'd never been happier. Likely, having all her children back in her home was the greatest Christmas present they could give to her.

"Now, now, dear heart." Hannah spoke matter-of-factly. "You already are a good wife."

"I'm trying—"

"In fact, not only should Weston be filling his own cup but he should also be the one tending to yours."

"It's alright." Serena poured a small amount of cream into Weston's mug, just the way he liked it—a fact she'd learned over the past weeks of watching him fix his coffee every morning. "I don't mind."

"That's the way Boone taught the boys—to look out for the needs of their women."

"I don't mind."

"No, no, no." Hannah began to bustle back to the kitchen door. "I'm getting Wes in here to do things right."

"Mrs. Oakley, please—"

"I insist you call me Hannah. Better yet, call me Ma."

Before Serena could stop the woman from making a fuss over the coffee, she disappeared into the front room.

"Wes!" Hannah's voice rang out. "Come here, son."

Serena pressed a hand against her forehead. She didn't want Weston to think she'd been complaining about him when all she'd been trying to do was be wifely and make sure he was happy.

The calls and conversation from the other room grew loud with teasing and instructions for Weston.

"Go on and kiss her again!" said one of the twins.

"Might as well take all the time you can get." The voice sounded like Maverick's.

Serena wanted to slink down and hide under the table, but as Weston was shoved into the kitchen, she held herself motionless.

He was grinning good-naturedly. Even so, mortification was rising swiftly within Serena, and she had no doubt her cheeks were coloring as a result.

At some point during the morning, Weston had groomed himself so that his hair was now neatly combed, and he'd donned a flannel shirt along with trousers held up by suspenders. He was as handsome as always, maybe even more so this morning—although she couldn't say exactly why. Maybe it was because he'd been smiling more often, especially during the gift exchange.

Now, as he came to a halt, he shot a glance her way, his expression filled with humor and a little embarrassment.

At least she wasn't the only one feeling the awkwardness of his family's matchmaking.

She held out the cup of coffee to him, the steam rising. "I just wanted to do something nice for you and didn't think I'd be stirring up trouble."

"Thank you kindly." He approached and took the mug. "But my ma is right, though. I should've been the one coming in and refilling your coffee."

She was just relieved the strain from their early morning kisses had dissipated and that Weston was back to interacting with her the way he normally did.

He took a sip, then gave her a grateful smile. "Next time, I'll be sure to take good care of you."

"You already are." And that was the truth. From the first day, when he'd driven her back to his home and searched for her horse, he'd done everything his ma and pa had taught him.

He set the cup of coffee down on the table, then stuffed his hand into his trouser pocket. He seemed to clutch at something there before pulling his hand loose. Then he stuck his hand in his other pocket and pulled out a small box tied with a red ribbon. "I was hoping I could get a minute alone with you to give you this."

He held out the box.

"This isn't necessary. Not after you've already given me so much." All month long, he'd constantly found ways to buy things for the house or for Tate or even for her.

He thrust the gift into her hands. "Of course it's necessary. It's Christmas morning."

She took it and fingered the satiny ribbon. She didn't want to keep comparing Weston to Palmer, but she couldn't stop herself. Weston was as opposite from Palmer as any man could get.

"Open it." Weston's voice rang with a note of eagerness, as though he truly cared about making her happy.

She tugged at the ribbon, and it unraveled and fell away. All the while, she could feel Weston's intense gaze upon her. What was he thinking about? Was he remembering their kiss from earlier? Was it vividly replaying in his head the way it was in hers? She wished she could study his face and decipher his thoughts, but she kept her attention on the gift.

With great care, she lifted the lid. There, on a bed of black velvet, was a gold necklace with a pearl at the center. It was gorgeous—and no doubt very costly.

"Weston." She breathed his name almost reverently. "You shouldn't have."

"I wanted you to have something nice."

"It's more than nice." This time she allowed herself to look up at him, finding him but inches away, his gaze upon her mouth, the dark blue swirling with hot sparks.

Was he thinking of kissing her again?

Her heart picked up speed. Did she want him to kiss her again? If it would be anything like the earlier kiss, then yes. She wanted it. Very much so.

Heat puddled low inside her belly—a delicious heat that made her want to press up against him and thank him with an embrace. Was this, then, what affection could be like between a man and a woman?

He was still staring at her mouth.

Should she tell him she would welcome another kiss? It was Christmas, after all, and their time of waiting had come to an end.

She couldn't be that bold, could she? But she also didn't want him to hesitate on account of her, especially if he was worried that she might not welcome him.

Surely there would be nothing wrong with giving him a hint that she wouldn't reject him if he did want to kiss more.

"Weston?" Her voice came out slightly breathless, and a flush moved into her cheeks at her brazen thoughts.

"Hmmm?" His voice came out a low rumble.

"I won't push you away—that is, if you want

to—I won't be opposed . . ." The heat flamed into her skin. She was stumbling over her words worse than a drunk stumbling down a street.

Weston didn't move or respond.

Had she misread the situation? Maybe he didn't want to kiss her after all.

Finally, he cleared his throat and took a step back. "Listen . . ." He glanced toward the kitchen door as if he couldn't get out of the room fast enough.

She turned to face the stove. "I apologize—"

"No, don't. I should apologize."

"It's alright. I understand." But did she? What was going on between them when one moment he seemed interested and in the next he was pushing her away?

"Done kissing in there?" came one of his brothers' calls.

Serena busied herself pouring another cup of coffee—this one for herself, even though she wasn't particularly in the mood for more.

"I guess I should get back." Behind her, Weston's tone was hesitant.

She nodded and forced cheer into her answer. "Of course. I'll join you in just a moment after I get my coffee ready."

A moment later, his footsteps crossed the

room and exited. Only then did she let her shoulders fall and a sigh escape from her lips.

Maybe she was letting her hopes get too high for her marriage to Weston. Did she need to keep her expectations more realistic?

After all, she couldn't forget that the good things in her life always seemed to come to an end. If she wasn't careful, she'd lose Weston. And she wasn't ready for that to happen.

Fourteen

He was acting like a stubborn pack mule on an uphill climb, and he had been the entire ride back to Fairplay.

With the midday sun breaking through the clouds as Weston dismounted in front of his house, he could feel Serena's questioning gaze on him the same as it had been for most of the journey. No doubt she was full to the brim with questions—namely, why he was putting off their intimacy.

He wasn't sure himself. All he knew was that he'd about died and gone to heaven kissing her in bed yesterday. When he'd landed back on earth, it'd jarred him so that he hadn't been able to get out of the loft fast enough.

Then there'd been that interaction with her in the kitchen, when he'd given her the Christmas present. The strength of his desire for her had nearly swamped him, especially when she'd hinted that she'd be okay with him kissing her again. He was embarrassed to admit he'd had half a mind to drag her out to the barn and kiss her senseless. In fact, he'd been real close to it. He'd been almost desperate to taste her mouth again.

But a part of him hadn't quite been ready.

As she started to slip from the saddle, he reached for her waist, fitting his hands on both sides of her. Her hips were just as soft and curvy against his hands as he'd imagined. And yep, he'd been imagining a whole heap about her since holding and kissing her.

Even though he'd tried not to, his mind had wandered there anyway—every blamed second it could.

Shoot. No woman oughta feel as good as Serena did.

He set her and Tate on the ground and found his hands lingering on her a mite longer than they needed to. Tate wiggled against her, ready to be down after the hours of sitting and ready to greet Ranger who was circling around them with wagging tail. Tate's motion forced Weston to release Serena, but not before she glanced up at him again, her eyes uncertain and maybe even a little anxious, as though she knew something was bothering him but was afraid to ask.

"Me hungry," Tate declared as he toddled toward the front steps, Ranger right by his side.

The little fella had stayed awake this trip and had been talkative and full of questions nearly the entire way. It'd left little time for Weston to talk privately with Serena, which he clearly needed to do.

He probably should've found some time yesterday to have a conversation with her. But after exchanging gifts, they'd sung carols, played parlor games, feasted on an enormous Christmas dinner, and ended the day by reading the Scripture account of the birth of Christ.

By the time the house had finally been quiet, Serena had already gone to bed with Tate.

Now, as Tate began to climb the porch steps, Serena chased after him.

Weston wanted to follow after her, didn't want to confuse or hurt her by his stubbornness. But he had to take care of the horses and check on how things had gone during his absence. Even so, he needed to say something eventually. He may as well say it sooner rather than later.

"Serena?"

She paused where she was holding Tate's hand as he attempted to climb another step. "Yes?"

"Reckon I need to do some jawing, if you've got the time." He forced himself to say the words, knowing he had to stop being a coward and face whatever was holding him back.

"Of course." Her eyes were solemn, and she set her lips into a straight line, as though she was already preparing herself for bad news.

He wasn't aiming to deliver bad news, was he? All he wanted to do was discuss what was happening between them. Maybe it was also time to tell her about Electra, his first love.

He waited for the stab in his heart that came at the thought of Electra. But strangely, he felt nothing—nothing but an angst to go after Serena right now and kiss her again. Serena was here in his life, more vibrant and alive than any of his memories of Electra from so long ago. Serena was the one who was his wife. Serena was the one he thought about day and night. Serena was the one he longed for more than he'd ever longed for anything else.

Not Electra. Not anymore.

And that was okay, wasn't it? After all this time since her passing, maybe he was finally moving the memories out of his heart and laying them to rest.

He patted his trouser pocket and the ring box. He'd wanted to give it to Serena yesterday on Christmas Day, but he'd held back and had instead given her the necklace.

She and Tate had given him a plaid wool scarf. He guessed she'd used the last of her earnings from the boardinghouse to be able to buy it for him, which made it even more meaningful.

The honest truth was, she was both beautiful and kind. There was no reason for him to hesitate in loving her. And he needed to allow himself— maybe even push himself—to move on.

He made quick work of unhooking their luggage from behind the saddles and emptying the saddle bags of everything his ma and sisters had sent home. He piled the goods on the porch outside the door, then led the two horses down the path behind the house toward the barns and corrals.

Dusty was in among the steers, clearing ice from the troughs. As Weston drew nearer with the horses, the cowhand straightened and pushed up his hat, revealing his roughened, scarred face.

Weston quickly surveyed his cattle, taking note of their condition, still as healthy and hearty as the day he'd left. "Much obliged to you for keeping an eye on the place while I was gone."

"Happy to do it." Dusty's normal smile didn't make an appearance. His expression was more serious than usual, making his droopy eye close up so that he looked like he was winking.

When Weston had passed by the mills and surveyed his place a few minutes ago, he hadn't noticed anything amiss. But that didn't mean nothin', since trouble had a way of creeping in without making a whole lot of racket.

He paused by the split-rail fence. "Something happen?"

Dusty lowered his axe and leaned against it. "Had an investigator come out this morning looking for your wife."

Whoa now. "What kind of investigator?"

"Said he was working for a man who goes by the name of Halifax."

Weston searched the corners of his mind for any recognition of the name. "Nope. Never heard of him."

"Apparently, Halifax is your missus's married name."

"It's Taylor."

Dusty shrugged. "Mr. Halifax says he's her father-in-law. Claims your missus ran off with Tate, and that Tate belongs to him."

A cold shiver that had nothing to do with the winter wind prickled the back of Weston's neck.

Dusty glanced around, and seeing no one else, he continued, but not without dropping his voice a notch. "Said that the new missus is an unfit ma, and that before passing, his son said he wanted Tate raised by him."

The shiver slid down Weston's backbone, and he peered at the house, the cheery curtains in the windows all new since Serena had come into his life. Was there a lick of truth to the news the investigator had brought them?

Weston held out the reins of both horses to Dusty. The fellow set aside his axe, climbed the fence, and hopped down. "Reckon that fellow is stringing whizzers together worse than a politician."

"Yep. He's an old windbelly telling a yarn." But even as Weston agreed with Dusty, the certainty smacked him clear in the face. Serena had been hiding something from him all along—

the real reason she'd come to Fairplay in the first place and why she'd agreed to marry him so quick-like.

Without another word he spun and stalked back to the house, his gut sloshing like it was full up with bad whiskey. It was time to get answers— maybe even past time.

As he reached the kitchen door and tromped inside, the sourness in his gut was lathered to a foam. He didn't pause to greet Maude, who was at the table slicing vegetables. He didn't pause to wipe his shoes or his hands the way Maude wanted him to. And he didn't wait for her scolding him as he crossed into the hallway. Instead, he listened for Serena—if that was even her real name.

Hearing voices and footsteps in the rooms overhead, he took the steps two at a time. As he entered into the hallway, he stopped short at the sight of her sitting on the floor with Tate in the bedroom, both still in their coats, Christmas presents from the family spread out around them. Thanks to Maverick, everyone had known about Tate and had been prepared with more gifts than one little boy needed.

Even so, it had warmed Weston's heart to see Tate so excited about the presents he'd opened on

Christmas morning. Even now, Tate was touching each item with great pride—the little wooden trains, the harmonica, a knitted cap and mittens, and a ball and cup game.

At Weston's appearance in the doorway, Serena and Tate looked up at him. "Play with toys, Pa?" The eagerness in the boy's voice tugged at Weston. Did Serena's father-in-law really have more right to the boy than Serena?

Instead of answering Tate, Weston nodded curtly at Serena. "I need to talk to you. Now."

She rose right away, her brow furrowing. "What's wrong?"

He motioned to the hallway. Their conversation wouldn't necessarily be private from Tate, but at least they could speak without constant interruptions.

She stepped out, her face still flushed from the cold of the long ride. She untied the ribbon of her cloak as she turned to face him, strands of her hair having fallen, and now dangling around her face.

"Who's Mr. Halifax?" He kept his voice to a whisper, but it still came out as hard as a nail driving into a metal beam.

She blanched and took a tiny step back,

clutching her cloak closed as if that could somehow protect her from his wrath.

"Don't lie to me anymore," he practically growled.

"I wasn't planning on it," she whispered. "I wanted to tell you, was going to tell you soon—"

"Who is he?"

"He's my late husband's father."

"And what's your real name? Is it Serena Taylor?"

"It's Anne Serena. And Taylor is my maiden name."

"So you're Anne Halifax?"

She jutted her chin. "I'm Serena Oakley."

He paced to the end of the hallway, swiped off his hat, and jammed his fingers into his hair. He should've known his marriage to Serena was too good to be true, should've known it would fall apart just like every other relationship he'd tried to have after Electra.

He stared up at the ceiling for several moments, then paced back to Serena.

Her eyes were round and full of remorse. "I'm sorry, Weston—"

"Does Halifax have the right to Tate?"

"No." The word came out hard. "Tate is mine. And I'll never let that man have him."

"He's saying your husband gave him Tate."

"Now that I'm married again, my father-in-law has no right to take my boy away."

Yep. This was why she'd been so ready to marry him. Because she'd wanted to find a way to protect herself and Tate from her father-in-law.

She'd used him, and that thought nettled him—although he had to quickly push aside the voice of reason that reminded him that he'd done the same thing, that he'd used her to appease his family.

Regardless, she'd lied to him about her identity, her reason for being in Fairplay, and why she wanted to be with him. Or maybe she hadn't exactly lied. Maybe she'd just left a whole lot of her story unspoken.

Either way, he had to get away from her and figure out what he was gonna do next.

"I'm going." He started toward the stairway.

She took a quick step after him. "Going where?"

"Reckon I'll ride into town and hear out Halifax and his side of things."

"He's a manipulative man," she called after him, no longer whispering.

"Manipulative? Really now?" He didn't bother whispering either. His question was loaded with insinuation. And it was unfair. But he was too angry to care. "I'll make up my own mind about that."

She didn't say anything more as he clomped down the steps and through the entry hallway. He shoved his way out the front door, and only then did he pause as he stood on the wraparound porch.

"Blast it all." He slammed his Stetson back on, pain riding his tail and shooting him full of bullets. He suddenly felt all out of air and energy, as if his lifeblood was draining from him. If he'd thought he'd been hurt by the other women who'd rejected him over the years, this pain couldn't even begin to compare. It was the worst yet, and he wasn't sure he'd be able to recover from it this time.

Fifteen

Weston stalked into the dining room of Hotel Windsor and aimed for the corner table where the proprietor, Mr. Fehling, had directed him.

"Mr. Halifax?" he called, not caring about the stares he was drawing from the few other patrons lingering past the noon hour. The dozen or so round tables scattered about the dining room were still laden with plates and bowls mostly scraped clean, and the scent of beef stew lingered in the air along with the haze of cigar smoke.

Two men lounged at the corner table, and now one of them shifted to take in Weston as he wound his way toward them. With spectacles perched on his nose, the fellow watched with too much curiosity and calculation to be anything but an investigator.

How had the man tracked Serena to Fairplay? Currant Creek Pass leading into the South Park basin from the southern part of the state would have been snow-covered but not impossible to navigate. Even so, not many hiked up into the high country this time of the year.

Weston crossed the last of the distance and stopped at the table with a nod toward the investigator before homing in on the other man, who had to be Halifax. With brown hair sprinkled with gray, the fella had a hardened face, tanned from days spent in the sun and filled with leathery lines around his mouth that his long mustache didn't hide.

He held himself with a casual air, leaning back in his chair, puffing on his cigar and peering out the window to Fairplay's main thoroughfare, which was nearly deserted at midday.

Even though the fella was acting as though he hadn't noticed Weston's approach, Weston knew his tall, brawny body and imposing presence were difficult to ignore. Besides that, his anger had taken on a life of its own during the ride from the ranch to town. Now, that anger was stomping around inside him like a battalion about to attack.

Serena might have hidden her true identity for Tate's sake, and she might have failed to reveal her problems, but one thing was certain—Serena was a good mother. Weston had seen it from the first time he'd ever watched her interact with Tate. And if Halifax was saying otherwise, then he was lying.

Halifax blew out another cloud of smoke before dangling his cigar over the ash tray on the table and setting it into one of the grooves. "You must be Mr. Oakley," he finally said, his voice holding the swagger of a bull.

Weston didn't have the patience for fellas who thought too much of themselves, and he sure in high heavens wasn't about to let a dandy like Halifax come to Fairplay and push him—or Serena—around.

"Heard you're making claims on my son." Might as well lay out the cards and see if this man could play a straight game or if he'd bluff his way through it.

Halifax pushed back from the table, his chair scraping, both hands on his revolvers at his waist.

Weston tensed and let his hands rest upon his revolvers too.

The investigator quickly rose and backed away. No doubt he feared he'd end up in the middle of a duel. No doubt he was right. Weston didn't have to be around Halifax longer than a few seconds to realize the man wasn't right for Serena or Tate. He guessed the man's son—Serena's first husband—hadn't been right for her either.

Not that Weston was necessarily the right man instead. But if her previous husband had been anything like his father, then it was all too easy to see her marriage had been miserable.

"May as well head on back to Pueblo, Mr. Halifax." Weston spoke loudly enough that everyone in the room could hear him clearly. He wanted as many witnesses to this conversation and his claim on Serena as possible. "I married your daughter-in-law, and she's mine now."

The honest truth of his own words hit him hard. Serena was his. She belonged with him. And he wanted her.

That didn't mean they wouldn't have some things to work through. That didn't mean their marriage would be easy. And it certainly didn't mean they wouldn't have problems cropping up again. But Lord in heaven above, he loved her. And really, that's all that mattered.

Yep. He loved her. Even if he was mad at her for holding back all this about her past, he reckoned he could understand why she'd done it when she was facing a difficult man like Halifax.

"You can have the woman." Halifax held on to the handles of his revolvers. "I don't need her. But the boy is mine, and I intend to take him home with me."

"Tate belongs to Serena."

"Tate belongs to my son——"

"Belonged. Your son's dead and ain't got a claim on anyone now."

"He told me I could raise Tate."

"A mother has the right to raise her own child. And there's not a judge alive who would disagree with that."

"They will when they learn how unfit she is."

Weston scoffed. "Everyone in this town has seen with their own two eyes what a decent and kind woman Serena is. Won't be a single person who'll say otherwise."

"Weston's right." A fellow at one of the other tables spoke up. "Never met a nicer lady in all my days."

Mr. Fehling had stepped into the room, holding a coffee pot. "She gave Christmas baskets to each of the mill employees, even though she hardly knew them."

"That's right," said another. "And she took

care of a sick old man out at the Courtney Boardinghouse and did a fine job."

"I saw her every week with her little boy in town," called someone else behind Weston. "And she was as sweet with him as could be."

Jericho Bliss, the Pinkerton agent who worked in the high country, hadn't said a word from his spot at another corner table, but he was watching Halifax intently.

Halifax's jaw twitched, as did his fingers. The man was lanky and wiry, full of muscle, and clearly a fighter, like most hard-working cowboys.

But Weston wasn't about to let the fella intimidate him. He braced his feet apart, willing to defend Serena's honor as well as her right to keep her son, even if he had to get hurt to do so. "Might as well admit defeat, Halifax. You heard only a handful of people praise Serena. You can bet the rest of the town'll say the same thing."

Halifax tipped up the brim of his hat. "She can have more children. Yours. But I'll never have anyone else."

Weston wanted to feel sorry for the fella, but he couldn't. Not after the way he'd threatened Serena, called her unfit, and had probably tried to take Tate away from her already.

Weston shrugged. "Someday when Tate's old

enough to make up his mind for himself, maybe he'll want to meet you. By then, if you work at it, you might be worthy enough to spend time with him."

"I'm not planning to wait that long."

Weston's backbone turned to steel, and he met the fella's gaze head on. "Stay away from Serena and Tate, do y'hear?" He couldn't keep the growl from his voice. "If you come anywhere near them, I'll make sure you regret it."

Without another word, he spun on his heels and started back toward the door. He wasn't sure what he'd do to Halifax if he showed up in Fairplay again. But one thing was certain. He planned to keep Serena and Tate safe, no matter what that took.

"Watch out!" Bliss, the Pinkerton agent, shouted and then a gun blast resounded behind Weston. He didn't stop to think. Instead he dropped behind the nearest table just as a bullet whizzed past him and crashed into the front window, shattering it.

Another shot came from the direction of Bliss, who was also down on the ground, taking cover behind a table but with his revolver out and pointed at Halifax.

The other men in the room were ducking, all except Halifax, who took aim at Weston again.

A blood stain was forming on the fella's shoulder, where he'd obviously taken a bullet from Bliss. Even though one arm was injured, Halifax squeezed the trigger of his second revolver.

Weston dove to the floor, narrowly missing another bullet.

Holy high heavens. Halifax wasn't messing around. No wonder Serena hadn't wanted to reveal her identity and chance having this man track her down.

Weston sucked in a quick breath, tossed a prayer heavenward, then rose and aimed, hoping he could hit and disarm Halifax before the man could hurt anyone else.

But Mr. Fehling had somehow managed to replace his coffee pot with a rifle. The hotel proprietor didn't hesitate. He pointed the barrel directly at Halifax and shot.

As the bullet hit its target, Halifax met Weston's gaze, his eyes bearing sadness and regret. Then the momentum of the blast threw him backward against the table he'd vacated. He crashed into it, then fell to the floor.

Halifax clutched his chest where the second bullet had hit him, blood rapidly seeping through his garments and turning his hands slick with crimson.

Slowly Bliss stood, one revolver still trained on Halifax and the other on the investigator, who had both hands raised in a show of surrender.

Weston pushed up until he was standing. He brushed his hand over his body, expecting to feel blood or a wound, but there was nothing. He was alive and unharmed, and suddenly all he wanted to do was ride as fast as he could back home and make sure Serena and Tate were alright.

After exchanging a few words with the Pinkerton agent, he strode from the hotel and was mounted and galloping hard north, need pulsing through him with such intensity he could hardly breathe.

He loved her. The words pounded through his head in rhythm with the hoofbeats. But he'd been a fool and had almost pushed her away. His pa's words from when they'd parted earlier in the day resounded in his head: *Serena's a good one. Don't sabotage this relationship like you have all the others.*

Weston had nodded but had let the advice slide right out of his mind, like he had all the other words of wisdom his father had given him. But what if his pa was right? What if ever since

Electra, he'd always been looking for ways to make relationships fail?

Maybe he'd been afraid to let himself love again for fear of losing. Or maybe he'd never believed he could love anyone the way he'd loved Electra.

Whatever the case, it was no coincidence that he'd failed at all his past relationships. Anytime something went wrong, he walked away.

Just like he was doing with Serena . . .

He'd been scared to give her his whole heart. Then, at the first problem that'd manifested itself, he'd done what he was good at—he'd pushed her away.

But the honest truth was that he loved her. That love had been building all month so that now it thrummed through him. The closer he got to home and to her, the stronger the need pulsed, so that he wasn't sure how he'd ignored it for so long.

Serena was everything he wanted and needed in a woman, and it was past time he told her that.

As he finally reached his land and raced down the lane past the mills, he didn't bother stopping to talk to any of his customers or employees. In fact, he didn't even wave a greeting. He headed directly for the house and hopped down before his horse came to a complete stop. He took the stairs two at a time, threw open the door, and started up the stairway.

"Serena?" he called.

The house was eerily quiet.

She was probably upset, and he wouldn't blame her if she didn't answer him.

"Serena, I'm sorry." His voice echoed loudly enough for her to hear, wherever in the house she might be.

As he reached the second floor, he stalked down the hallway, his boots clunking loudly. He glanced first in Tate's room and then in his and Serena's. She wasn't in either, and there was no sign of Tate.

Weston raced back to the stairway and stopped short at the sight of Maude at the bottom, her wizened brown face set into a scowl.

"Where's Serena?" He almost couldn't get the question out because he dreaded Maude's answer.

"What do you think?" Maude fisted her hands on her hips. "She and the boy left you."

Sixteen

Serena dug her heels into Belle, urging the horse into a faster gallop. Only one thought charged through her—she had to get away from Mr. Halifax before he caught her and took Tate from her.

"No, Ma!" Tate's sobs reverberated against her. From his spot in front of her in the saddle, he wiggled as if he had every intention of sliding down. "Me go home."

A lump formed in her throat. It wasn't their home anymore. It couldn't be. As much as they cared about Weston and loved living there, she had to find a new place where she and Tate would be safe from the reaches of Mr. Halifax.

Besides, Weston didn't want her there. She'd

had the feeling he was hesitant to love her. Now he was angry that she hadn't revealed the danger she and Tate were facing from Mr. Halifax. In the end, maybe Weston would be glad their marriage hadn't worked out.

"Please, Tate." Serena tried to hug the boy and comfort him as best she could. "We have to go away."

"Me want Pa!" His wail rose above the thundering of Belle's hooves, and it echoed in the grassland that spread out around them, dead and dry and deserted, not a creature in sight—not even the gophers.

"Pa can't go with us." Serena didn't know where they should run to next, but she found herself heading back up the road toward Hoosier Pass and Breckenridge—the same gradually inclining road she'd traversed a short while ago on the way back to Fairplay.

Weston's family had been so loving. Would they let her stay for a day or two until she could decide where to go and what to do next? Surely Mr. Halifax wouldn't track her there, would he?

"No, Ma. No." Tate's voice echoed with brokenness, slicing into Serena. She didn't want to hurt Tate by tearing him from Weston. Not after how quickly he'd grown attached to his new pa. Clearly Tate had sensed how genuinely Weston had cared about him. And that had helped Tate cling to her less and had even made him less afraid of new people.

After such progress, could she really take Tate away?

Even if Weston was angry with her for the deception, he was an honorable man and wouldn't cast her out. He'd also never collude with Mr. Halifax to take Tate away. Weston wouldn't be so cruel. It wasn't in his nature.

Besides, she'd done nothing wrong, and surely after thinking about it, Weston would realize that.

She'd done nothing wrong . . . except that she was running away like a coward . . . again.

Her hold on the reins loosened, and Belle immediately sensed the change in her intensity and slowed her gait.

Tate pushed away from her embrace. His cheeks were streaked with tears, and his nose was running. "Me love Pa."

She swallowed the swell of emotion that continued to clog her throat. "I love him too." She'd never loved a man before—at least, not the way she'd grown to care about Weston. And she didn't want to run away from him, didn't want to leave him, didn't want to lose him.

She wanted to spend her lifetime with him, learning to love him even more.

She tugged on the reins, bringing Belle to a halt.

Was it time to stop running away from her problems and instead stay and fight for her marriage? Maybe she needed to fight for her right to keep Tate too. She hadn't been a bad wife or a bad mother.

Yes, she'd need to apologize to Weston for deceiving him. She should have told him about her situation right from the start. But she was strong enough to stay. She was strong enough to fight. And she was strong enough to be a good wife to Weston.

In fact, maybe she'd been a good wife to Palmer too. After being with Weston and experiencing his kindness and consideration to both her and Tate, it was easier to see Palmer's insufficiencies. What if the problem hadn't been her? What if it had been him?

"Go home?" Tate peered up at her expectantly, as if sensing the resolve beginning to course through her.

If she ran away every time trouble came riding after her, she'd be teaching Tate to do the same. And she didn't want him to be a coward.

She wanted him to learn to fight against adversity.

She veered Belle back around so that she was facing Fairplay. Yes, she'd let herself believe she wasn't enough for too long, and it was time to stop. She guessed that it wouldn't always be easy and that she'd still have many days when she doubted herself.

But today she could start by talking to Weston and telling him everything about Palmer and her time living with the Halifaxes.

"Let's go home." She kissed Tate's forehead, and he smiled through his tears.

She nudged Belle into a trot. As she rounded the riverbend and the open prairie spread out before her to the south, she caught sight of a lone figure on horseback riding hard in her direction. A man in a black Stetson, with broad, muscular shoulders that contained enough brawn to wrestle a bear.

Weston? What was he doing riding north? Was he coming after them?

Her heart gave an extra beat at the prospect. But she quickly forced herself to think realistically. He'd been angry with her. He deserved her apology. And he might need more time to learn to love her the same way that she loved him.

Either way, she needed to tell him she wasn't running away from him or their marriage and that she wanted to work through their issues.

"Serena!" His shout wafted across the barren plains.

At the sound of Weston's voice, Tate sat up straight, searching all around eagerly. At the sight of the horse and rider, he began shouting. "Pa! Pa! Me love Pa!"

Tears sprang into Serena's eyes. Weston was all too easy to love. It hadn't taken Tate long to love his new Pa. And it hadn't taken her long either.

"Me love Pa!" Tate shouted again.

Weston was rapidly closing the distance, his horse thundering powerfully.

Serena reined in, her fingers suddenly trembling. She prayed desperately that, at the very least, he'd listen to her, give her the chance to explain herself.

As he reached her, he jerked his horse to a halt. His jaw was clenched in tight lines. His brow was furrowed beneath the brim of his hat, and his blue-black were eyes filled with angst.

He slid down from his mount and came straight toward her, strength radiating from each hard step. "Serena—"

"Me love Pa." Tate held out his arms toward Weston.

Weston didn't hesitate for a second. He lifted Tate down from the saddle and into his arms, and the little boy went to him eagerly, wrapping his arms around Weston's neck.

Weston hugged him close, and Tate laid his head on Weston's shoulder, the stiffness dissipating from the little body as if he'd finally reached the place he wanted to be.

Tears sprang to Serena's eyes at the sight of her boy with such a man. This was one reason, among many, that she'd fallen in love with Weston: he was so tender and loving to Tate.

"I love you, too, little fella." Weston planted a kiss on Tate's head against the knitted cap covering his pale hair.

"Me go home." Even though Tate's words were muffled against Weston's coat, they reverberated through Serena.

She hadn't really had a home since leaving Oklahoma. But since the day she'd moved in with Weston, she'd felt as though she'd come home.

"I ain't letting you go." He hefted Tate closer, but his gaze locked now with hers. "You're mine now. And you belong with me."

Her heartbeat spurted forward. Was he talking to her now too?

"I'm sorry, Serena." His eyes held hers. "Or should I call you Anne?"

"Serena." The new name seemed fitting for the newer and stronger woman she wanted to become.

He nodded. "I should've never doubted you for a single second."

"I should have told you the truth right away, and I apologize."

"You had a real good reason for keeping quiet. And even if you didn't, I should've reacted differently, with a whole heap of patience."

"But I wasn't honest. Even that night when we got married, I purposefully set out to meet you on the road. I let Belle loose because I wanted a chance to see if I should add you to my possible-husband list."

He reached out a gloved hand and stroked Belle's muzzle. "Reckon I owe Belle a favor, then."

Serena's breath hitched. What did he mean? Wasn't he frustrated with her for more deceitfulness?

He glided his hand over Belle for another second before reaching for Serena's hand, still on the reins. He circled his hand around hers. "The honest truth is, I've been holding myself back from love for a long time. For the past eight years, to be exact—ever since my fiancée died."

His fiancée had died?

Weston met her gaze frankly. "She was out rounding up stray cattle when a winter storm struck. She got lost . . ."

How tragic. "I'm sorry, Weston."

"She never made it back to Breckenridge to her family's ranch. I didn't even know she'd gone missing until it was too late."

"I can't imagine how hard that must have been."

Weston nodded, swallowed hard, then took a deep breath. "I've been hanging on to her for too long. But since meeting you, somehow I've finally been able to let go. And you're the one I'm wanting to hold on to now."

The air inside her remained stuck. Could he really be saying what she thought he was?

"I was trying to fight my feelings for you, trying to protect myself from getting hurt. But it hurts more to think of you not in my life at all."

"But I don't want to bring you into the middle of all my problems with my father-in-law. He is a dangerous man—"

"*Was* a dangerous man." Weston's expression turned solemn. "When I rode into town, I told him to leave you and Tate alone. Reckon he didn't like me telling him what to do, so he started shooting at me."

"Shooting at you?" She scanned him, her chest tightening. "Did he hurt you?"

"I'm fine. Not even a scratch."

Weston had defended her and Tate to her father-in-law. She should have trusted him, should have known he'd see the truth of her situation.

"Turns out the other fellas came to my defense. And when I left town, Mr. Halifax was breathing his last."

She slumped in the saddle, relief weakening her. She knew she ought to feel some sadness for the man who was Tate's grandfather, but she was only glad that, finally, she'd no longer be in danger of losing Tate to him.

The afternoon sunshine was lending her some warmth, but she shivered anyway.

Weston tugged at her hand, and she dismounted so that she was standing in front of him. Tate was still clinging to him and probably wouldn't let him go anytime soon.

Weston didn't seem to mind. In fact, he was still holding Tate just as tightly. "What I'm trying to say is that I love you. I love you more than I ever thought it possible to love one woman."

A soft sob swelled and escaped before she could stop it. Quickly, she cupped her hand over her mouth to catch any more emotion. But even as she did, her eyes brimmed with tears.

The hardness was gone from his face, replaced by earnestness. "I want you to come back so that I can prove my love to you today and every day for the rest of my life."

This time a tear escaped.

His brow began to furrow. "Please, Serena. You don't have to feel the same. I promise that I'll do my best to love you enough for the both of us."

"You don't have to do that, because I already do love you."

At her declaration, the shadows in his eyes fell away.

She couldn't bear to be apart from him for a second longer. She stepped toward him and wrapped her arms around him. Even though Tate's little body prevented her from hugging Weston completely, she sidled into the crook of his body.

For a long moment, he held her with one arm and Tate with the other. Finally, Tate began to wiggle, and Weston broke away from her to set the boy down on the road.

"Me ride with Pa?" Tate grabbed the dangling reins of Weston's horse.

"Yep. You can help me, little fella." Weston reached for Serena's hand. "But first, I want to give something to your ma."

Before Tate could question him, Weston lowered himself onto one knee before her. He pulled a small box from his pocket, then he lifted the lid and held it out to her. "I was a fool for not giving this to you earlier. Can you forgive me?"

The beautiful rose-gold band shimmered in the sunlight, revealing a pattern of twisted vines that surrounded an opal. It was exquisite, and she loved it because it was from him. "Of course I can forgive you. I just hope you can forgive me too."

"Done."

"Thank you." She tugged off her mitten and then gave him her hand.

Gently, he slipped the ring down her finger. "I'm claiming you, sweetheart. Now you're mine."

As he settled the ring into place, all the love that had been growing for this man swelled within her. She wished she had something to give him in return, something that would show him just how much she wanted to claim him too.

She could think of only one thing. She tugged at Weston, drawing him back to his feet. Then she pulled him toward her and captured his mouth with hers. She didn't have much to give, but she offered him a kiss that was filled with all her passion . . . and with the promise of all that was yet to come.

Thank you for reading *Claiming the Cowgirl*. I hope you enjoyed Serena and Weston's love story!

Keep reading for a sneak peek at my next sweet historical romance, *Waiting for the Rancher*, the first book in the High Country Ranch series, featuring Weston's brother, Maverick Oakley.

HIGH COUNTRY RANCH SERIES
WAITING
FOR THE
RANCHER
JODY HEDLUND

Waiting for the Rancher

HIGH COUNTRY RANCH SERIES | BOOK 1

Summit County, Colorado
April 1879

"Can't believe she's really gonna marry a scallywag like you." Maverick Oakley punched his best friend's arm. "She must be desperate."

Sterling Noble straightened his black string bow tie. "What can I say? I'm irresistible."

Maverick stuck a finger into his own bow tie and loosened it. Even then it still felt like it was strangling him, just like it had since the moment he'd put it on.

They stood side by side in front of the bureau mirror in the room Sterling had always shared with his brothers. Maverick was an inch or so shorter than his friend's six feet three inches, and he had leaner facial features with a square jawline and more prominent chin. His hair was darker—almost black—compared to Sterling's lighter brown, and he had blue eyes while Sterling's were brown.

Other than that, they both had rugged, muscular frames that came from years of hard work on their families' bordering ranches. Their skin was weathered from the sun and wind of Colorado's high country. Although most of the time they had a layer of scruff on their jaws, today, on Sterling's wedding day, they were both clean shaven.

Sterling was staring at himself, his eyes wide and filled with trepidation.

Maverick gave his friend a nod. "Violet's real lucky. You're a good man, the best. She couldn't ask for anyone better."

Beneath his collar and tie, Sterling's Adam's apple rose then fell. "Hope I can make her happy the way she deserves."

"You will."

A light rap sounded on the door.

Sterling didn't move, continued to examine himself as if he were counting his flaws and all the ways he didn't measure up.

"Come in." Maverick took charge for his friend, guessing he'd be nervous on his wedding day too. Not that he was getting married anytime soon. He hadn't cared about women, not for months. Not since his pa had died. He actually hadn't cared a whole heap about anything. Even today, he was having a hard time mustering the appropriate enthusiasm.

The door opened, and Hazel stepped into the room. "You fellows ready?"

Sterling's kid sister had her hair done up in a fancy style, with what appeared to be little pearls woven throughout. She was wearing a silvery gown that shimmered in the spring sunshine that was pouring through the room's tall window.

Maverick wasn't used to seeing her all gussied up. Most days at work, she wore her sturdy corduroy skirts, tall leather boots, a duster coat over a simple blouse, and a hat with her hair tucked up out of sight.

Even though he'd seen her nearly every day since she'd taken the position of broodmare manager last autumn, he rarely got a view of her fair hair, blond like a light-colored sorrel.

With her forehead puckered, her bronze-colored eyes swung between him and Sterling. "What's wrong?"

"Nothin'." He answered for Sterling, clamping his friend on his shoulder and squeezing. "We were about to head downstairs."

Hazel didn't respond, the sure sign she didn't believe him. That was the thing about Hazel—she could read emotions in people and animals better than anyone. It's what made her so good with horses and why his pa had hired her.

Maverick stuck a finger into his collar again, that familiar strangling sensation returning. His pa wouldn't be at the wedding today because of him and his foolishness. His pa wouldn't be at any event ever again, big or little, important or not.

An ache swelled in Maverick's chest, and he drew in a quick breath to try to push it back down.

At his intake, Hazel's gaze softened. He hadn't told her what he was feeling, hadn't shared about the remorse that was turning into self-loathing, but he suspected she knew, almost as though she could visibly see his pain and understood why the day was hard for him.

Giving himself a hard mental shake, he grasped Sterling by the shoulder and began to guide him toward the door. "Let's go, big fella. Time to get hitched."

Sterling went along willingly. "Reckon you're right."

Hazel moved into the hallway and waved them ahead of her. Sterling took a step, but then paused in front of the door across the hall, where Violet was getting ready with her sister and mother.

She was perfect for Sterling in every way. He'd been crazy about her since the day her family had moved to Breckenridge and he'd first laid eyes on her a year ago.

The trouble was that Violet didn't adore Sterling to the same extent—at least, from what Maverick could tell. She was a real nice gal and all, but there were times when Maverick wasn't sure she was ready to settle down.

He'd been surprised when Sterling had proposed marriage to her a few months ago, especially since the two hadn't been courting all that long. But Maverick had supported Sterling the way any best friend would. In fact, he'd even helped Sterling with his proposal plans, the plans they'd made when they'd been younger and had dreamed up how they'd each propose to the woman they fell in love with.

Sterling had decided he would propose by taking his true love skiing to nearby Devil's Glen, have a romantic dinner in an old miner's cabin there, and then ask her to marry him during dessert.

Maverick had been the one to ski out to the cabin ahead of time. He'd set up everything, including table linens, candles, and pine boughs to freshen the scent. He'd even brought the meal the Nobles' family cook had made. Maverick had ensured that every detail was perfect.

The January day had been beautiful, and the conditions had been just right. Sterling had proposed to Violet the way he'd always planned. The problem was Sterling had taken Violet by surprise, and she'd turned him down. He'd come back from the monumental event crushed.

The next weekend, Violet had apologized to him and accepted the proposal. Course, Sterling loved her enough to put aside his disappointment and had given her the ring again.

Now with the coming of April, the big day had arrived.

Sterling hesitated in the hallway. Was he thinking of stopping and talking with Violet?

Maverick steered him away from the door. "Naw, you don't get to see her yet."

Sterling shuffled forward. "Just wanted to talk

to her through the door and make sure she's all right."

"Everything's fine." Maverick gave him a shove. "Now c'mon."

Sterling nodded, as though trying to convince himself that everything really was fine. Then he started down the stairs, and Maverick trailed him with Hazel on his heels.

Family and friends were milling about in the entryway of the Nobles' sprawling ranch house. The double doors leading to the front parlor were open, revealing more guests waiting for the start of the ceremony.

In years past, Maverick's whole family would have been at a gathering like this. His pa and ma and five siblings. But today . . .

His gaze snagged on his twin sisters, Clementine and Clarabelle, who were seated on a settee just inside the parlor where they were chatting with Mrs. Noble. Besides himself, they were the only Oakleys at the wedding. And Clarabelle had almost stayed home because she hadn't wanted to leave Ma's bedside.

Ma's pale face and listless body flashed to the front of his mind. Not only had his foolishness cost Pa his life, but it was costing Ma hers too.

She was dying of a broken heart, and with each passing day, she was only getting worse.

Sterling finished descending amidst warm congratulations, but Maverick paused near the bottom of the stairway and swallowed hard.

What was more, without Pa there, the family was falling apart, and it was all because of him.

Maybe he hadn't been directly responsible for all that had happened to cause the big rift between Ryder and Tanner, but if Pa had been there, he would have known what to do to make them see reason. In fact, his two younger brothers probably wouldn't have started fighting at all, not with Pa intervening and bringing about peace.

At a gentle hand on his shoulder, Maverick shifted to find Hazel on the step above him. Her warm gaze seemed to encourage him that everything would be all right.

But he knew the truth deep inside. Nothing would ever be all right again.

He pulled at his tie, loosening it another notch. Even then, his breathing turned shallow, and he couldn't seem to get enough air.

With franticness rising inside, he glanced around for an escape and locked in on the front door. He needed to step outside . . . for a few seconds.

He broke away from Hazel's hold and descended the last couple of steps. "Be right back." He tossed her what he hoped was a grateful look. "Need a fresh lungful."

She was peering at her mother, who was motioning at her to hurry. "Don't take too long. Everyone is waiting for the wedding to start."

He was already winding his way past the guests to the front door. Although he was tempted to remind Hazel he wasn't holding things up, that Violet and Sterling were the ones dallying, he bit back his comment and pushed out the door.

He stepped onto the wraparound porch that faced Bald Mountain and the range lining the eastern part of Summit County. The rocky peaks were covered in a thick layer of snow that the high-altitude sun was slowly beginning to melt away.

The pasture spreading out in front of the Nobles' house was still barren and brown with patches of snow piled in the shade of boulders or brush. Hints of green were beginning to make an appearance, but it would be another month before blue grama grass began to flourish again.

As he crossed the porch and started down the steps, he sucked in a deep breath of the cool air.

The dampness of soil and the waft of cattle and manure filled his nostrils.

He wasn't ready for the wedding, wasn't ready to be around everyone, wasn't ready for going on with life as if everything was the same as it had always been when it had all changed.

He followed the flagstone path forward several feet. Then he halted and inhaled again, his sights on the towering range ahead. If only he could be as strong and solid as the mountains, just like his pa. But he was all too often hotheaded and hasty.

Squaring his shoulders, he stuffed his hands into his trouser pockets. As he swept his gaze over the beauty of the wild mountain valley, the sadness in his chest spread into his limbs. Although he loved the high country, no one had loved it more than Pa.

For the past fourteen years since leaving their horse farm in Kentucky, Pa had done everything he could to build a new life for his family in Colorado. After years of hard work, Pa had finally begun to see the rewards of his efforts. The High Country Ranch—or High C Ranch, as it was called—had gained a reputation for having the best horses in the state, possibly even in the West.

Maverick gave a shake of his head, as if that

could somehow shake away the melancholy. He couldn't make today about him and his sorrow and regrets. This was Sterling's special day, and he had to be there for his friend and not stand outside feeling sorry for himself.

He shifted to return inside, but at the sight of a woman in a cream-colored gown leaning against the side of the house, he paused. The dark hair and pale skin were all he needed to recognize Violet.

What was she doing outside?

She had a handkerchief out and was blotting the corners of her eyes, almost as if she were crying. What was wrong? Was she having pre-wedding jitters?

An urgency prodded him. He couldn't let Sterling see his bride like this, outside, crying. It would only make him more nervous.

Maverick shot a glance toward the front door, then to the parlor window. He could take care of this without Sterling being any the wiser. He'd talk to Violet and encourage her to go in right away and proceed with the wedding.

He veered off the path and strode across the flat tufts of grass. The dampness muted his bootsteps so that he was almost upon Violet before she glimpsed him nearing.

She pushed away from the house and rapidly began to dry her cheeks. "Hi, Maverick."

He stopped a foot away from her.

She averted her face and continued to blot at her eyes. "What are you doing out here?"

With his hands still stuffed into his pockets, he gave a slight shrug. He couldn't very well admit that he'd been overcome with guilt over his pa and family. She didn't need to hear that today. "Came lookin' for you, darlin'." The words were out before he could stop them. "Wanted to make sure you're okay."

She lifted her eyes, which gave him full view of the angst clouding them. "I don't know what I'm doing."

"I do. You're gonna go in there and marry the man you love."

"But how do I know if I really love him?"

How could she not love Sterling? The fellow was one of the kindest and most giving men Maverick had ever known. "Listen—"

"What if I have feelings for someone else too?" She straightened and seemed to pull in a steadying breath.

"You're just nervous. That's all."

"No. It's not all." She blinked back more

tears. "I haven't been as sure about Sterling as he's been about me."

Maverick's gut cinched. He was glad Sterling wasn't nearby to hear the confession. "Don't matter none. Sterling's got enough love for the both of you." That was the plain truth. Sterling had been a goner since the day he'd laid eyes on Violet.

"I don't want to hurt Sterling." She pressed a hand against the long row of covered buttons that ran up the front of her bodice until she reached the brooch at the neckline. "But I just don't think I'm ready for this."

This conversation wasn't going the way Maverick wanted, and he had to do something—anything—to assure Violet that Sterling was the right man for her. He scrambled to find a solution. Maybe he oughta pick her up and carry her inside.

Without giving himself—or her—a chance to protest, he bent and swept her up into his arms. "C'mon. I'm taking you back in."

As he situated her against his chest, she wrapped her arms around his neck. Her skirt was full and the layers of material cumbersome, forcing him to hold her closer to keep from dropping her. He rounded the house and headed back toward the front door.

Her arms tightened with each step, and she lifted her head so that her cheek brushed against his. "Please. We need to talk."

At the plea in her voice, he halted. He dropped his gaze to find that she was looking up at him with furrowed brows. She was such a pretty woman. Not that he was attracted to her, but that didn't mean he couldn't admit she had stunning features, with pale skin that made her eyes and hair all the more vibrant.

"You're a good man," she whispered.

"Course I am." He offered her what he hoped was an encouraging smile.

She studied his face, ending up at his mouth. "You have such a nice smile."

"So do you, darlin'." He let his smile widen, hoping he could cheer her up. "I'd sure love to see your pretty lips smile right about now."

Her eyes only welled with more tears. "Oh, Maverick."

"I said I wanna see your smile, not tears." He gentled his voice.

"I think I have feelings for you too." Her arms tightened around his shoulders.

"Whoa, now." What was going on here?

Her gaze trailed his face again. "I've tried to ignore the feelings, but they just won't go away."

"Don't go saying things like that." He lowered his voice to a hiss. This was bad. Real bad. Worse than bad.

"You can't deny you've been feeling things for me too." Her fingers at the back of his neck crept into his hair.

He had to fix things quick-like, before the situation went downhill even more. "Now darlin'—"

She rose up and pressed her lips to his, cutting him off. Her mouth was soft and her kiss filled with desperation. Her hands in his hair dragged him down, and at the same time, she deepened her kiss.

Maverick couldn't move. The shock of the moment paralyzed him. What was Violet doing? Why was she kissing him? And how could he help her see the error of her way? Help her realize the only man she oughta be kissing was Sterling?

At the banging of the front door and Sterling's shout, Maverick's heart plummeted. No doubt his friend was witnessing this whole interaction with Violet.

Maverick's muscles stiffened. He couldn't let Sterling find out the truth, that Violet had been the one to initiate the kiss. It would break his heart.

There was only one way to keep Sterling from suspecting Violet had cheated on him. Maverick pressed into her. He'd take the blame for the kiss, act like it was his idea.

The instant he let his lips fuse with hers, he knew the plan was foolish, that it wouldn't work. That he couldn't kiss her in return, not for any reason. But before he could pull back, Sterling was grabbing his arm and wrenching Violet from him.

Get your copy now!

Author's Note

And that's a wrap! I hope you enjoyed *Claiming the Cowgirl*, the final book in my Colorado Cowgirl series. Even though this series has come to an end, this won't be the last time you'll get to see familiar characters and definitely not the last trip to Colorado.

Weston's five siblings are ready and eager to find true love, so grab your horse, climb into the saddle, and journey with me to Summit County and High Country Ranch for more exciting adventures and sizzling romance with the Oakley family.

Each of the siblings have a story of their own and a chance to find true love, starting with Maverick Oakley. *Waiting for the Rancher* is available now and I hope you loved the sneak peek!

To stay up to date on all my books, visit my website at jodyhedlund.com. Or join me and other readers in my Facebook Reader Room at facebook.com/groups/jodyhedlundsreaderroom.

About the Author

 Jody Hedlund is the bestselling author of more than fifty novels and is the winner of numerous awards. Jody lives in Michigan with her husband, busy family, and five spoiled cats. She writes sweet historical romances with plenty of sizzle

A complete list of my novels is available at jodyhedlund.com.

Would you like to know when my next book is available? You can sign up for my newsletter, become my friend on Goodreads, like me on Facebook, or follow me on Twitter.

The more reviews a book has, the more likely other readers are to find it. If you have a minute, please leave a rating or review. I appreciate all reviews, whether positive or negative.

facebook.com/AuthorJodyHedlund

instagram.com/jodyhedlund

x.com/JodyHedlund

pinterest.com/jodyhedlund

bookbub.com/profile/jody-hedlund

amazon.com/stores/Jody-Hedlund/author/B003JLXD6A

More Colorado Cowgirls by Jody Hedlund

Committing to the Cowgirl

After years away, Astrid Nilsson has returned home to Colorado, hoping to become Fairplay's second doctor and to find healing for her reoccurring consumption. Dr. Logan Steele is seeking to hire a male physician to take over his clinic after he goes back East. When Astrid, his childhood sweetheart, insists that she's the one for the job, he offers her a bargain she can't refuse: pretend to court him to appease his mother and he'll give her the doctor position on a trial basis.

Cherishing the Cowgirl

Charity Courtney is at her wit's end trying to save her boardinghouse from a bank foreclosure. Wealthy railroad magnate Hudson Vanderwater hears of Charity's plight. Although he comes across as cold and callous, he is drawn to helping women in need because of a tragedy that destroyed his sister. He concocts a plan that will save Charity—he'll employ her and rent her boardinghouse for the month and in doing so alleviate her debt.

Convincing the Cowgirl

When unexpected visitors arrive at the Courtney Boardinghouse and claim the place belongs to them, Patience Courtney finds herself homeless and penniless. When wealthy rancher, Spencer Wolcott, proposes a marriage of convenience, Patience accepts the arrangement. In exchange for a new home, she agrees to become the mother to Spencer's precocious little girl so that he can manage his prosperous ranch.

Captivated by the Cowgirl

Now that her sisters are both married, Felicity Courtney manages the Courtney Boardinghouse alone. After nearly collapsing from exhaustion while caring for an invalid man and his wife who are staying at the boardinghouse, Felicity posts an advertisement for a hired hand. Philip Berg, a prince in disguise, is hiding in Fairplay while attempting to stay one step ahead of an assassin. When the spirited Felicity Courtney tacks up a notice that she is hiring help, he offers to do the job.

www.ingramcontent.com/pod-product-compliance
Lightning Source LLC
Chambersburg PA
CBHW032259310726
48973CB00008B/2464